The Name Was Stash

I told Floyd Chilly my name, T.D. Stash, and he asked "What's the T.D. short for?"

"Only my mother knows," I said. "And she's not talking. Most everyone calls me Stash. Or worse."

Then I gave him the spiel. How I was a fishing guide by trade, not a licensed investigator. How I now and then agreed to undertake a search and rescue for valuable goods, human and otherwise, for which, if successful, I was given an agreed-upon fee. How I advised potential clients to go to the authorities unless there were compelling reasons not to.

Floyd Chilly dismissed the mumbo jumbo with a wave of his hand. "What my lawyer told me was that you-all knew just about everything goin' on in these parts, most especially of a shady nature. And if anybody can locate my boy and get him out of his trouble, you're the one."

I allowed that I was. That was my first mistake. . . .

THE NEON FLAMINGO

A T.D. STASH CRIME ADVENTURE

BY W.R. PHILBRICK

AN ONYX BOOK

NEW AMERICAN LIBRARY

NAL BOOKS ARE AVAILABLE AT QUANTITY DISCOUNTS WHEN USED TO PROMOTE PRODUCTS OR SERVICES. FOR INFORMATION PLEASE WRITE TO PREMIUM MARKETING DIVISION, NEW AMERICAN LIBRARY, 1633 BROADWAY, NEW YORK, NEW YORK 10019.

 Onyx is a trademark of New American Library

SIGNET, SIGNET CLASSIC, MENTOR, ONYX, PLUME, MERIDIAN and NAL BOOKS are published by NAL PENGUIN INC., 1633 Broadway, New York, New York 10019

First Printing, November, 1987

1 2 3 4 5 6 7 8 9

PRINTED IN THE UNITED STATES OF AMERICA

For Tom Skelton,
who knows where the fish are,
and for Lynn,
who knows a good book

1

SHE had the best bottom in Key West, and I wanted her bad. I had a Barlow knife in my hand and a wad of greenbacks in my shirt pocket. I was ready to lie for her, to fight if necessary. This was love, as true as it gets.

The pink coral sand was hot under my sneakers. Intense sunlight bleached the scraggy landscape. Beyond the cove the aqua-blue Gulf was languid and oily, the horizon blurred with heat distortion. A faint breeze wafted in, thick with the humid stench of mangroves. Even the stunted palms that bordered the boat yard were drooping in the heat of noon.

I stood in the shade of her hull, poking the knife in the keel seam, telling anyone who might be interested that it was too bad about the dry rot. I was lying about the dry rot. Her bottom was perfect.

"Sweet lines," I said. "You don't let a little ketch like this go, not if you've got the time to rebuild her. I plan to tear out the garboard and the stem—probably the transom, come to think—and replace any piece that's punky. Three, four years, I'll have her good as new."

The ketch I had the hots for was an H-28, one of old Francis Herreshoff's classic designs. Cedar on doubled oak frames, copper-riveted. Pretty as a picture and ideal for single-handing. All it needed was a coat of bottom paint and about five days to swell

tight, and then I figured on drinking around the Dry
Tortugas, tuning up the rigging, and getting the feel
of the tiller. Provided I was the only serious bidder
in the red-tag auction of vessels seized by the DEA.

"A labor of love," I mused, loud enough to be
overheard by the other bidders. "That's what she
deserves. I figure maybe eight, nine hundred hours."

I was talking to the air. *Audacity*, the big twin-
engined Y & G cruiser, was getting most of the
attention. With her go-fast hull and the turbo-charged
diesels and a spacious, open cockpit she was built
either as a rich man's fancy or as a dope runner's
dreamboat. She'd already been the latter, and now
the DEA auctioneer was hoping she'd revert to the
former. Looking over at the crowd of good old boys
gathered under her fat transom, I wasn't so sure.
Too many Vuarnet sunglasses and heavy gold neck
chains. By the time the gavel came down there was
an even chance *Audacity* would be headed for another cargo of "square grouper." Inside a month
she'd probably be burying her waterline with an
offshore load of the Colombian weed that keeps the
keys afloat on a sea of smuggler's booty.

It's a game they play down here at latitude 24. It
goes something like this: an enterprising fisherman
leases his boat out for a midnight run, at a fee that
will replace his vessel and then some. If it blips on
the DEA radar screen or the Coast Guard gets nosy,
the crew abandons ship—into a cigarette boat that
just happens to be standing by, say—and after impounding the vessel and the illicit cargo, said vessel
goes on the block. Someone else buys the naughty
boat and it's off to the races again.

It's one way of keeping the money in circulation.
I'd been in the business myself, briefly. I got out one
step ahead of the guy with the big iron key, the one
who wanted to lock me up in the Raiford Country

Club for a couple of years, or ten. Now it was the straight life for T. D. Stash. I made my living honestly.

Well, sort of. Mostly.

Now and then I strayed, although not to running bales. What I did, I had a nice little skiff customized into a guide boat. A builder I know fit it out with a live well, a beer cooler, a 140-horse outboard, a fiberglass pole to push her through the shallows, and a seat cushion up in the bows. Now and then the seat cushion is covered by someone who is willing to pay my day rate to go stalking the shallows for bonefish or tarpon or a 'cuda big enough to be interesting. The guide boat gig is for walking around money. When I need a new pair of sneakers I do other things, of which more later.

"You can put away the knife. No one's paying you any mind, Stash old buddy."

One of the gold-chained Vuarnet boys was standing right behind me, grinning at the back of my head.

"Hansen," I said. "What the hell are you doing in that get-up?"

Kurt Hansen, Lower Keys Operations Manager of the U.S. Drug Enforcement Agency, grinned under the designer sunglasses. He was wearing a ratty Conch Republic T-shirt, faded jeans, and rubber thongs. He had the deep, burned-in complexion of a man who spent a lot of time out on the water, or wanted it to look like he did.

"I'm blending in," he said, fingering the gold around his neck. "Camouflage."

"You might's well hang a sign on your back: NARC WORKING."

"That hurts," Hansen said, "coming from an honest citizen like yourself."

"I am but a poor fishing guide."

Hansen snorted. "My ass. You got plans for the

ketch? Last goofer owned it tried to scuttle her when the CG came alongside off the Marquesas. No charts, hadn't the faintest idea where he was. Fogged up with the fumes, *comprendes?* Had her so jammed with bales she wouldn't sink, even with the sea cocks wide open."

"Not exactly an ideal vessel for that game."

"So? Last week they got a goofer off Marathon, bringing in a bale on his windsurfer. Broad daylight. I tell ya, Stash, there's something about this business that addles the mind."

There were a couple of somethings. Unlimited cash and unlimited cocaine. A lot of the boys got bit by the crystal whiteness. Some it turned mean, some it turned stupid. One thing for sure, any smuggler who powdered his nose would end up lifting weights in Raiford Prison, sooner or later.

"So," Hansen said, eyeing the crowd near the *Audacity.* "You going to bid for this here sailboat?"

"Thinking on it."

He wished me luck and moved off, thumbs hooked in his jean pockets. The wharf-rat costume wasn't bad but Hansen wasn't fooling anyone that counted. Any more than I was, with my tall tale about having to take her down to bare wood.

The auctioneer arrived in a pickup, trailing a cloud of marl dust. A big guy with sloped shoulders, a barrel neck, and a smooth Everglades drawl. He stood on the bed of the truck, using an electric bullhorn, relying on an assistant who kept track of the bids. Out of curiosity I timed him. It took him exactly forty-eight seconds to knock the big Y & G down. Two hundred and ninety-five thousand dollars. Not bad for less than a minute's work.

As the new owner and his pals swarmed over the power cruiser, the pickup lurched over to where I was standing in the shadow of the ketch. The auctioneer looked down and grinned, showing off gold incisors. I could see the hot blue sky reflected in his sunglasses.

"Who gonna bid on this purty little thang?" he said, not bothering to switch on the bullhorn. "You?"

I shrugged and tried to look like I wasn't in love. A couple of good old boys wandered over to watch the show. One of them, a young trap fisherman, was in the business. If he wanted to give me a run for my money, it would be no contest. At a look of inquiry from me he spread his hands and shook his head.

"Last thing I want's some old wooden sailboat," he said. "If it ain't got a big diesel, I don't drive."

The auctioneer clicked on his bullhorn. In it the faint breeze from the mangroves was amplified into the breathy rush of fifteen-knot trades. I imagined myself at the helm of the H-28, tacking for the Dry Tortugas. Right about then Lily Cashman arrived. She was wearing a lime-green linen suit and she'd taken off her heels to walk over the rough gravel of the yard. I remember the heels because she kept raising one of them. In about thirty seconds she slipped the ketch right out from under me.

"Sold," the auctioneer drawled. "To the lady in green."

The truck moved off, spitting marl dust at me.

Lily tried to make it up to me over crab claws and beer. We were out on the wharf, having lunch at the Laughing Gull, an open-air tiki bar. Sitting in the shade of the thatch roof and listening to Jimmy Buffet on the juke. Dipping the sweet, cold crab meat in Dijonnaise sauce and washing down all that delicious cholesterol with Kirin, a Japanese beer I like to order because the dragon on the label is pretty.

"You can still have the boat," Lily said, licking her

fingers. "All you gotta do, take over the defaulted mortgage and pay the penalty fees."

"That's all, huh? And where do I get that kind of money?"

"Stash honey, don't take that hurt tone with me, okay? I am merely the attorney of record for the finance company. The auction of the attached property was only a formality. If you'd read the fine print in the notice to liquidate, you'd have realized there was a lien on that sloop."

"Ketch."

"Whatever."

Lily was in her mid-thirties. She was slim and trim. She had, as the saying goes, good bones. Auburn hair going sun-blond at the ends. Eyes that matched the lime-green suit, and a faint spray of freckles over the crisp line of her nose. She was exactly my type, but there was no reciprocal spark. From Lily's point of view I was the wrong gender.

"I've been trying to run you down for the last couple of days," she said. "All I get is that dumb recording on your answering machine."

I stared moodily at the water below the wharf. There was three fair-size barracuda down there, snouts into the current, poised like the interconnected segments of an underwater mobile. Things of beauty with a stillness and grace that made them almost invisible to the untrained eye.

"Why I called," Lily said, signaling for another basket of claws. "There's a job if you want it."

"I'm just a lazy conch wharf rat, Lil. Why would I want a job?"

Lily smiled, dabbing her sauce-buttered lips with a paper napkin. "There's only one reason," she said. "Money. You want that little sloop or ketch or whatever it is, you need cash. I have a client who will pay you for services rendered."

"Do I have to wear a suit and tie?"

Lily shook her pretty head.

I tossed a crab-claw shell into the water. When the shimmers cleared, the 'cuda had vanished.

"Okay," I sighed. "Tell me about it."

2

A Cuban shrimper limped into the basin, her rusted outriggers high, diesel thumping. A group of black-haired women stood on the dock opposite the Laughing Gull, most of them holding infants as they waited for their menfolk to bring the shrimper alongside. The men on the boat were grinning and holding their thumbs up, a sure sign that they were iced to the top of the hold with a good catch.

"What we're talking," Lily Cashman said, "is a filial recovery."

"Speak English. Or Spanish. Anything but legalese."

"Graham Chilly is among the missing," Lilly said. "Running with a bad crowd, his stepfather suspects. A wharf rat like you ought to be able to lay hands on him in a day or two."

I held the cold bottle of beer against my forehead and closed my eyes. "Drugs," I said. "I'm getting a psychic message that this missing kid is somehow involved with drugs."

Lily snorted and lightly tapped my bicep. "Some psychic. Ever hear of a kid in trouble down here who *isn't* involved with drugs?"

I held the bottle to my ear and pretended to listen. "Message received. Over and out." I put the bottle down and snuck a crab claw out of Lily's basket. "So

who are the parents," I said, "and why haven't they
gone to the relevant authorities?"

Lily winked at me from behind her photo-rays.
Law schools have special classes in how to avoid the
direct answer, and she had graduated at the top of
her class. After palming a quarter off the bar she
sashayed over to the jukebox. When Jimmy Buffet
had finished his cautionary tune about changes in
latitude, Lily slipped the coin in and punched a
combination. As she came back to her stool, the
intense sunlight reflecting off the water made her
linen skirt translucent. Fine legs with an interesting
apex. She caught me looking and stuck out a pink
tongue.

"Don't tell me it's a waste," she said, bumping
her knee against mine. "Sam doesn't think so."

Sammie is a diminutive, redheaded imp who runs
a windsurfer concession at Smathers beach. When
intoxicated Sam likes to show off her tattooes, one of
which is a heart with Lily's name inscribed. The two
of them had recently set up housekeeping on what
Lil hoped was a permanent basis.

"So," Lily said, "have you figured it out yet?"

"Figured out what?"

She jerked her thumb at the juke. "Who's singing
'Jail House Rock'?"

I wasn't in the mood for Name That Tune, but I
humored her by saying Elvis Presley.

"Listen again," Lily said, showing a lot of her
white teeth.

"Right," I said after a moment. "Not Elvis. Someone trying to sound like him."

"You got it," she said. "Famous Floyd Chilly in a
nutshell."

I smiled and tried not to look confused.

After giving me the lowdown on Famous Floyd

and his troubles, Lily dropped me off at my bungalow. I took a long cool shower that helped clear my
head of the dragon beers, then walked along the
northern shore back to the boat yard. The light was
just beginning to slant low off the Gulf when I got
my '67 Coupe de Ville going on at least seven of its
eight cylinders.

The coupe is a typical keys cruiser, with its fat
tires and sun-bleached finish, tattered rag top, and
the ring of rust around the rear bumper where wet
fishing gear has leaked from the trunk. Everyone
has a list of priorities. A new car is way down on
mine, well below a certain Herreshoff ketch, a lawn
chair that doesn't fold up when I try to sit down,
and a mirror for my one-speed bike. Besides, the
coupe has a habit of back-fire belching at just the
right moments.

The Chilly estate was on Palmetto Key, on the
other end of the Stock Island Causeway. Not many
keys estates are visible from the highway and the
Chilly place was no exception. I tried a couple of
gated entrances before finding a security guard who
acted like he was expecting me. The badge on his
shirt pocket looked fake, but the Magnum in his
holster was real enough.

"Park in the lot behind the main house," he said.
"An' doan block the drive, okay?"

The guard, a skinny Cuban with a pockmarked
face, was not impressed with the coupe. I could tell
by the way he held his nose as he waved me through.
There was a long curving drive over bleached marble
chips, through a grove of tall royal palms, painted
white at the base to keep out the chiggers. The lawn
was the kind that comes as rolled-up turf and is
hellishly difficult to maintain down here. Scuff your
heel anywhere in the string of islands that sprinkle
out from the bottom end of Florida and you'll strike

coral or limestone, which means that without a whole lot of costly site modification the drainage is poor. As I drove slowly by, a crew of gardeners was busy making sure that Floyd Chilly's turf stayed the color of new money.

I parked the coupe out of sight, where it wouldn't clash with the landscape. The estate house was perched on stuccoed stilts. Say that fast three times and you win a Monroe County real-estate license. The idea, any new residence has to be nine feet above sea level, the maximum estimated height of the floodwaters sure to follow in the wake of the next big hurricane, whenever it comes. Personally I'll take my chances on the roof of my old bungalow— there's something about lifting the underbelly of a house to the eye of the wind that's troubling. If the impending big one blows hard enough, there's a chance some of these new stilt places will go flying off to Kansas, along with the shorefront condos built on filled-in mangrove swamps.

A flight of precast steps took me up to the entrance. Stuccoed walls and lots of darkly tinted glass, all on one level. The white roof tile looked as if it had been bleached and scrubbed recently. I pushed the buzzer. It played a tune I didn't quite recognize.

Famous Floyd answered his own front door. He was wearing double-knit trousers the color of Key-lime pie—that is to say pale yellow—and a wide white belt that matched his patent-leather shoes. The long mournful face and the watery blue eyes looked familiar, but it was the pencil-thin mustache that clinched it.

Rock-a-Billy Hit Parade, Famous Floyd Chilly Sings Greatest Hits, Floyd Chilly's Golden Oldies. Order Now. Have Your Visa or MasterCard Ready. Not Available in Stores.

Such was the manufactured fame of late-night television record promotions. Call Now, Our Operators Are Standing By. The catch, if you cared, was that Chilly sang the greatest hits of *other* recording artists, not his own. He didn't sing his own hits because he didn't have any.

"You the gentleman Miss Cashman called about?" The voice was a soft Kentucky drawl, deeper than a barrel of sour-mash whiskey.

I told him my name and stuck out my hand. He shook it slowly, studying me.

"What's the T.D. short for?" he asked.

"Only my mother knows," I said. "And she's not talking. Most everyone calls me Stash. Or worse."

"Y'all come on out to the patio, we'll get acquainted. Reggie'll be back pretty soon, she'll want to talk at you."

I thought I detected a twinkle of humor in those sad blue eyes. It was hard to tell.

He led me through an arched doorway into a tiled hallway and around to the back, where a staircase curved down to a screened-in patio. There was modern wicker furniture that somehow gave the impression the designer had been trying to reinvent the porch rocker. I eased myself down into a chair. Floyd Chilly rubbed his hound-dog nose and sighed.

"Y'all wanna beer? Got a big pitcher of ice tea here, you'd rather."

I voted for the iced tea. It came in a tall sweating glass, with a mint leaf impaled on a plastic toothpick.

Chilly settled into the seat opposite and lifted his glass, gazing impassively at me over the rim. "I quit on the hard stuff a while back," he said. "You a drinkin' man, Stash?"

"Now and then."

"I was. In an extreme way. That's how I happened to meet Reggie. Twelve years back, before I got the mail-order thing going, they booked me on this second-rate pub tour over there in the U.K."

He drank deep from the glass, then wiped his knuckles across his lips. He stared out through the screens, where a hedge of bougainvilleas were in bloom. "Last thing I remember, me and the drummer they give me, we was raisin' some kind of hell in this hotel outside of Liverpool. Sucking down Scotch and eatin' them little red pills? Bad news. I woke up in the hospital. Regina was the nurse they put on me. Purtiest little thing I ever did see, Reggie. Well, the pub tour got canceled, of course, and the limey promoter diddled me out of what little I had coming. When I sobered up it appeared I was plumb broke. Not even a ticket home. That's a lonesome situation, you can't hardly raise the cash to get yerself home."

Nurse Regina, who didn't know rock-a-billy from "Rock of Ages," took him in. She kept a roof over his head until he got straightened out, and not surprisingly, nature took its course. Chilly's deep voice found an easy rhythm as he spoke; this was obviously a story he'd told before, many times over.

"What happened, Reggie and I got hitched. She had a husband had run off, left her with a boy. Graham. Nicest little fella. After we got married I took out papers on the boy. You go by blood, he ain't no kin, but we been real close, Graham and me, right from the start."

In the shade of the patio the tea in his glass looked a lot like whiskey. I chewed on the mint leaf and tried to guess how many years Floyd Chilly had etched in his leathery face. Mid-fifties at least. His hands were big and raw-boned, a farmer's hands. From what Lily Cashman had said, he'd retired to the keys with a fair-sized nest egg, and royalties from the novelty record albums that were still being sold through promotions on late-night television. Most of the nest egg had gone into the estate, comprised of the sprawling main house, various outbuildings, and three acres of prime Gulf waterfront. He was using what income he had to leverage an ambitious condo scheme on the other end of Palmetto Key. Vacation time-share. A risky, expensive business that could either pay off in a big way, or collapse in a saturated market.

"I'm worried sick about the boy," Chilly said, his voice a husky whisper. "He's got himself in some kind of trouble and it's probably my fault, I didn't try hard enough to talk him out of it. Miss Cashman said maybe you could help find him."

I gave him the spiel. How I was a fishing guide by trade, not a licensed investigator. How I now and then agreed to undertake a search-and-rescue for valuable goods, human and otherwise, for which, if successful, I was given an agreed-upon fee. How I usually worked through an attorney, which gave me an ambiguous and temporary investigatory status in the eyes of the law. How I always advised potential clients to go to the relevant authorities unless there were compelling reasons not to do so.

Chilly nodded, dismissing the mumbo-jumbo with a wave of his hand. "Yes, suh, Miss Cashman give me the same rundown. What she *did* say, under all those fancy words, was you-all knew just about everything goin' on in these parts, most especially of a shady nature. She tell me, Miss Cashman did, that if anybody can locate Graham and get him out of his trouble, you the one."

I managed to avoid preening and asked him what kind of trouble his stepson was in, how long the boy had been missing.

The rough farmer's hands tapped nervously on the arms of his chair.

"Three nights ago Graham was sitting right where you are now. Understand, he's gonna turn eighteen in a couple of months, which makes him an adult, but in a some ways Graham is a lot younger than that. He tends to get real excited, worked-up-like. Youthful enthusiasm, I guess you'd call it. Naturally he knew all about how we'd gotten ourselves into this condo deal pretty deep. Heard his ma and I scratchin' it over. We had to find refinancing once already and now it looks like we got to go back and refinance all over again. I won't bore y'all with our money worries, Stash; the point is, Graham was tryin' to help out. He had some kind of scheme cookin', an' he told me about it, and the fact is I wasn't payin' sufficient attention, or I'd a damn sure figured a way to dissuade him."

Somewhere beyond the bougainvilleas an air-exchange unit switched on. The mechanical hum was keyed low enough that it was almost subliminal. There was the sound of tires on fine gravel. Someone had arrived. Floyd Chilly sat up straighter, then slumped. "Reggie's home," he said. Not exactly overjoyed.

"Let me see if I've got this right. You think your stepson is putting together a drug deal?"

Chilly nodded. "That's what I'm afraid of. Graham sat right there and told me not to worry, that there was plenty of extra cash in Key West and he knew a way to get a chunk of it. I think what he said, he said he could find a 'temporary fix.' Fact is, Stash, the boy has a habit of talking big and nothin' ever come of it. Just the way he is. Hell, seems like *everyone* down here like to talk big, when it comes to runnin' drugs or knowin' someone who does, and I figured Graham was just lettin' off steam. Then he took off about midnight in that Camaro we give him for his birthday. He ain't been back since."

"He ever do this before," I asked, "stay away for a few days?"

Chilly shook his head. He seemed to be listening, waiting for steps to fall. "Now, I ain't sayin' he never come back late. He done that now and then, rolled in around noon, lookin' like he been raisin' hell. But this time, just before he took off, he come up and give me a bear hug and say, 'Don't worry, I got everything all set.' He ain't as much as phoned since then."

"Mr. Chilly, I'll ask around, do what I can to see if we can scare up Graham. Meantime I think you should contact the sheriff's department, see what their reaction is."

Chilly leaned forward in the chair, eyes on the stairway as he whispered, "Just between you and me, Stash, I done that already. Went over the afternoon after he didn't show. The boys over there, they checked the hospitals, just in case Graham cracked up that fast car of his. No sign of him, nor the Camaro. Only thing else they can do is put out an all-points. I ask 'em if that means they'll undertake a search, they say no. Too many runaways down here. All-points just means they'll take him into protective custody and notify me if they happen to stumble on him. Which ain't happened yet."

"You mention that Graham might be involved in a drug deal?"

"Hell no. But wouldn't you know, that's the first thing those boys assumed?"

It was the first thing anyone would assume, south of Tallahassee. I heard someone on the stairs and saw a remarkable thing happen. Floyd Chilly's face underwent a rapid transformation, as if he had slipped on a mask.

"Well, hel-*low*, honey bunch," he said heartily, his voice projecting welcome. "This here is Mr. T. D.

Stash, the gentleman Miss Cashman was telling us about? Stash, this is my wife, Reggie."

Mrs. Chilly glided over the patio and gave me her hand. There was a faint scent of orange blossoms. She was small-boned and slender, wearing a flowing chiffon pantsuit that showed off her tiny waist. Bare shoulders and arms peeked through here and there. Her complexion was pale, considering how sun-drenched was the world she now inhabited. Early forties, perhaps, but artful application of cosmetics enabled her to pass for a decade younger.

"How good of you to drop by, Mr. Stash." Her clipped accent, softened only slightly by immersion in the American South, conveyed the idea that despite our great difference in height, it was she who was looking down on me. Releasing my hand, she said, sweetly, "I hear you know every two-bit crook from Marathon to Key West."

"Now, Reggie," Floyd said.

Regina Chilly ignored him, focusing slate-gray eyes at me. A smile flickered at her lips. "Well," she said softly. "If anyone wants to know what I think, I think my son has run off with a girl, or perhaps he's at one of those wild orgies I keep hearing about, the ones that last for days? I am not persuaded that he's been kidnapped by pirates, or whatever Floyd has been telling you."

"Reggie, sweetheart . . ."

With a demure wave good-bye and a hydraulic pivot of her hips, she glided back up the staircase. As put-downs went, hers was pretty classy, good theater.

"Pirates, Mr. Chilly?"

The old rock-a-billy crooner sighed. "Let's take us a walk, Stash. I'll show you what I found in Graham's bungalow. You can see for yourself."

A crepuscular light washed through the tall palms.

Ahead of us the purple waters of the Gulf splashed sunset up against the green felt shore.

In the picture a thin, fair-haired boy was crouched next to a television set. He was grinning shyly and pointing at the television. The image on the screen was blurred, indistinct: an album cover with an 800 number dimly displayed under it.

"Graham would have been ten years old. That was the year we went back to Nashville, the year I cut that deal for the Greatest Hits promotion. Geez, he was real excited about that, Graham. He's seen me do my club gig, and heard a couple of oldies on the radio, the low-watt rock-a-billy stations, but seeing me on the boob tube, that made it real for him."

Floyd Chilly was sitting on his stepson's cot, hands folded in his lap. The bungalow windows were open. The incandescent orange ball of the sun was plunging into the Gulf. Out on Mallory Wharf the sundowners would be going through the motions, cadging coins from the tourists, trading drugs, exchanging lies, and lice.

"When did Graham move out here?" I asked, looking at the rock posters tacked to the walls, a model airplane suspended from a thread, a Martin acoustic guitar with a broken string.

"Oh, sometime last year, I guess. This was supposed to be the guest cottage, but we don't have many guests, an' if we do there's plenty extra rooms in the big house. What the boy wanted, I assume, was a measure of independence. Without actually moving away and setting up on his own."

"Maybe what he wanted," I said, "was a place to snort coke unobserved."

Chilly nodded glumly, staring down at his folded hands. "Well, yes," he drawled, "the notion occurred to me, after I saw what he had in that drawer."

Chilly had taken me out to the bungalow, located on a spit of land not far from his private dock, to show me his stepson's cache of drugs.

"I come out here that morning he didn't come home," he explained. "I don't know what I expected to find. Not that."

In the bureau was a shoebox. In the shoebox was a glass vial with about a half an ounce of cocaine and a deck of carefully sealed envelopes, each containing a quarter-gram of the powder. Thirty envelopes in all.

"These go for twenty-five bucks," I said, holding up one of the small envelopes. "He sells all of them he'll have grossed seven hundred and fifty bucks. Depending on how much he cuts the stuff, he'll make four or five hundred in profit. Take about an hour on any weekend night."

Chilly raised his eyes and stared at me. I got the distinct impression he didn't like me judging Graham by the contents of the shoebox.

"I know the scene, Stash, okay? Musicians was screwing around with coke and a lot of other stuff, too, way before you was a sparkle in your daddy's eye. Back when I was still working a band, in the 60's, it was meth was the big thing, crystal speed. Now it's cocaine. Maybe next year it'll be something else. But it's always there, whatever it is. Hell, I'd a been surprised the boy didn't try a little of the stuff, just for the sake of experiment. What troubles me, he was obviously dealing."

"Obviously."

"Street-level dealing, Stash. Nickel bags. Okay, they cost more now, but it's the same damn thing." Chilly stood up, gazing out the bungalow window at the color-splashed show in the west. "It wasn't he needed the money. We give him a good allowance."

"Maybe he thought *you* needed it?"

Chilly turned from the window, shook his head. "What, a few thousand bucks? We're lookin' for half a million, keep the project afloat. Graham knows that."

"So he's out trying to turn the big trick? Bring in a load?"

Chilly shrugged. "Find him for me, okay? Before he winds up in jail. Or dead."

I closed the bureau drawer and found a recent picture of Graham Chilly, a class portrait. He was thin enough so his ears stuck out. In the left lobe was a small hoop earring that failed to make him look mature. He had his mother's face and her light, clear complexion, although not her cunning. That was worrisome. If he was trying to float a major transaction, he would need cunning, a whole lot of it. And luck. On the way back we made a sidetrack to the private dock. A thirty-foot Challenger was tied up to the float. Custom-built up in Marathon and rigged for sports fishing, with a fighting chair and the big side whips, and an elevated steering station perched above the flying bridge. There was a pulpit on the bow, and a harpoon lashed to the stanchion. The goldleaf lettering on the transom caught the last blaze of the sunset.

"I'll make you-all a trade," Chilly said. "The boat for Graham."

He extended a hand. We shook on it.

GOLDEN OLDIE
Palmetto Key, Fla.

3

MUTT Durgin runs the wharf at Land's End, where I keep the *Bushwhacked*, my little guide boat. Mutt handles the fuel and supplies, sells bait, rents fishing gear, books the occasional client for me, and is one of the four or five best liars in Key West. He claims to be a swamp cracker from the Everglades, but when he's in his cups, a funny twang slips into his voice that makes me think he's from the Jersey Shore. He denies this vehemently. I do know that when he first showed up in the keys he had a pint-sized gator he walked on a chain, and a parrot that rode his shoulder. In those days he had a gold hoop in one ear and hair on his head, and tourists were understandably interested in snapping his picture, what with the bird and the reptile and all. Mutt would charge for the privilege. He had a pretty good thing going until the gator developed an insatiable desire to have the bird for dinner. Mutt lost his cool when he saw the beast burping parrot feathers, dispatched it to gator heaven, and found himself in need of a new gig.

He claims to have won his section of wharf in a card game. Who knows? It might even be true.

Mutt was in his shack when I got there, feet up on the crawfish trap he keeps for effect, drinking Caribaya rum out of a paper cup. He was smoking a cigar that

had never cleared customs and listening to the
weather report on his citizen band.

His chamois-brown skull swiveled in a fog of blue
smoke. "You lookin' for work?" he said around the
cigar.

I said what I always said in response to Mutt's
eternal question.

"No way, no how."

"Stash, you are the laziest man in the Florida
keys."

Coming from Mutt Durgin, that was high praise
indeed. He removed the cigar from his mouth and
tapped a crisp white ash to the shack floor. He was
wearing a sleeveless T-shirt that was lettered FISH OR
CUT BAIT. He favored the sleeveless look because it
showed off the musculature of his powerful arms,
about the only part of him that wasn't grizzled and
wrinkled and scarred by the sun.

"Snowbirds in town," he said. "You want to make
a day's pay? I only suggest this because you are at
present a month overdue on your dock fee."

"Impossible."

"I ain't pushin', darlin'." He grinned, setting the
cigar back in the corner of his mouth. "I'm full
aware what a trauma it is for you to exert yourself to
the extent of taking a snowbird out and letting him
hook onto a tarpon."

I dug into a jean pocket and extracted the crum-
bled wad of bills that hadn't been enough to buy the
ketch. Mutt took the dock fee without comment and
rang it up. He opened a ledger by the cash register
and made a mark against my name. When he turned
back I held out the snapshot of Graham Chilly.

"Ever seen this kid?"

Mutt studied the picture. "So that's it. You're back
in the business," he said, pronouncing it "bid-niss."
"Well, he *does* look familiar. One of those faces you

see around town. He may be in with that bunch that hot rods around the canals, bustin' up Daddy's speedboat."

"Graham Chilly," I said. "Ring any bells?"

He shrugged, settling back into his wooden chair, crossing his boots on the crawfish trap. Without asking, he held out a paper cup with a shot of the rum.

"Go on," he grumbled when I hesitated. "Improve your health."

"His father—stepfather—is Famous Floyd Chilly."

"Famous Floyd, huh?"

"As seen on late-night TV. Got a time-share condo scheme over on Palmetto Key."

"Hell, yes," Mutt said, grimacing as he downed the run. "Now I gotcha. Heard the project was in some kinda trouble. That's the kid, huh? Yeah, I seen him, can't remember where."

"Recently?"

"Last few days. Maybe a week by. Along in there. What'd he do, run away from home?"

"Something like that. You see him, or hear anybody who has, let me know."

Mutt nodded agreeably and waited for me to empty the paper cup. I did. He smiled contentedly and burped. Fire-breathing dragons must feel like that, after they've torched a questing knight. Eyes watering, stomach churning, I put Graham Chilly in my hip pocket and headed west along the waterfront.

Twilight lingered on Mallory Wharf. Just about everything lingers on Mallory Wharf, including a cast of scruffy characters who look like they've wandered off the set of a *Twilight Zone* episode about the Lost Tribe of Hippies. Some of them were actually there at the beginning, in Haight-Ashbury. Several will claim to have been on the bus with Ken Kesey.

That famous bus, fueled by free LSD, never got anywhere near the keys, but the wise thing to do is nod agreeably; to argue or doubt such tales is to encourage an even longer version. There are stories that were begun on Mallory Wharf years ago and have not yet ended, stories that are interrupted only for ingestion of hallucinogens or febrile attempts at copulation. One of these never-ending stories calls himself Fletcher Brown. It might even be his real name.

"Yup," he said, squinting at the photograph. "That's Gram."

"Graham?"

Fletcher grinned. He does not have an excess of teeth, although his gums look healthy. He keeps his long gray hair in a ponytail and looks and smells reasonably clean.

"They call him Gram. Kid gives it away."

Fletch, who's been in Key West almost long enough to qualify as a native conch (we say it "conk" down here), picks up a couple of honest dollars each season helping to haul in trap lines. The rest of the time he hangs out, selling a few neatly rolled numbers to the sailors and tourists who flood the town. The heat leave him pretty much alone. As a vendor of such small aspirations—three bucks a joint—he's considered at worst a tolerable pest, of no more nuisance value than a palmetto bug. He's got a line on just about every street creature and drifter that floats through, and a memory that, astoundingly, has not been affected by the more or less continual inhalation of the potent weed he sells.

"Not a bad kid, Gram, but messed up in a weird way," he said. I paid attention—someone had to be seriously disturbed to be labeled "weird" by Fletcher. "Carries a pocketful of quarter-grams, and all you have to do, hang out with him for a little while, he'll pass 'em out. No charge. Gratis. All he wants, people to like him, I guess."

"He *gives* the stuff away?"

Fletcher nodded. In the dim blue light his pale cat eyes seemed to have an inner illumination.

"A couple of thousand years ago," he said, "when I was in grade school, there was the kid on the playground, he'd give me a penny if I promised to be his friend. It's like that with Gram Chilly, sort of. Only nowadays a penny won't do it."

"But the toot will?"

Fletcher was sitting on the seawall, rocking on his skinny haunches. He had a nose with real, well, nobility, or size. Anyhow, there was a lot of it. His profile would not have looked out of place on a coin of debased currency. A thin swaggle of silvery whiskers hung from his mottled chin. Uncle Sam on acid.

"What it'll do," he said, thinking it over. "It will gather a crowd. You're giving away free toot, you'll never lack for companionship."

"Girlfriends?"

He shrugged, twining the beard wisp through his slender fingers. "The usual hangers-on. Chicks trying to make the scene, looking for a free score. Naw, wait a sec, there was one. A little older. I remember thinking at the time poor little Gram had a crush on her."

"Name?"

He shook his head, the ponytail swinging from shoulder to shoulder. "Sorry, never picked up on the name. Artistic type. Crashes in a houseboat over Coral Canal way. I don't think she gave the kid a tumble, but I could be wrong." A tightly rolled joint appeared in his right hand. His left cupped a match. He scratched it against the seawall and bent over the flame. A familiar, acrid scent resonated in the still

air. "Gram's old man is the old geezer on TV, right?
Hawking records?"

"Famous Floyd, Not Available in Stores."

"Yeah," he inhaled deeply, then exhaled with a
sigh. "Well, I remember one of the kids made fun of
old Famous Floyd. Did a takeoff on one of those
corny ads? Man, Gram really flew off the handle.
Tried to punch the kid out. Well, they pull him off
before any blood got spilled. I say to him, Right on,
man, stick up for your own. I ain't kiddin', Stash, I
thought he was going to burst into tears. Strange
little dude, always talking ragtime, but like I say, not
really a bad kid."

"Seen him lately?"

Fletcher thought about it. "No," he said. "Not for
three or four days. Last time he was down here, he
was tryin' to run something by Zach Malone. Zach
had that big Bertram of his tied up over there, and a
couple of his heavies ran little Gram right off it."

Malone was a hometown boy, a conch, the genuine article. Once upon a time he was elected as a
deputy sheriff. Then he was unable to explain why
there was eight tons of baled marijuana under a
tarpaulin in his garage and he got signed up for a
two-year hitch at Raiford. Since then he'd smartened
some. He now used other people's garages, and
other people's boats. The vacation in Raiford hadn't
lost him any friends, many of whom still jammed
into the saloon he kept on the north end of Grinnel
Street, and guys like Kurt Hansen at the DEA
figured him for a major transporter. A teamster. He
didn't actually sell the product, but he made sure it
got from Point A to Point B. I knew Zach slightly
and could not see him taking a kid like Graham
Chilly seriously. Chasing him off his boat would be
right in character.

"Gram show his face around here, I'd appreciate it you give me a ring. Or leave a message with Mutt."

"He in trouble?" Fletcher tucked my twenty into his little suede stash bag without looking at it.

"The idea is, I want to save his ass before some ornery old grizzly like Zach Malone has him for breakfast."

Fletcher offered me a hit. I wasn't in the mood. On the way back to Mutt's to get the coupe I passed twenty bars, easy. I wasn't in the mood for that, either. The music was loud and cheap. The laughter drifting from open doorways sounded like broken glass, sharp and with an edge of menace. I was in one of my moods. I went home to my bungalow and went out on the back porch and slipped into the hammock I've got strung up there. I lay with my hands behind my head, listening to palmetto bugs crash against the screen, and sirens in the distance, thinking about a ketch with the best bottom in Key West and a troubled boy who tried to buy friendship with little white envelopes.

They've been trying to run the houseboats out of the keys for a while now. The fact that there are people who figure out ways to live that do not involve putting down roots or paying taxes is galling to an average home owner. It's irritating to think that anyone who can scrape up a couple of hundred dollars can float a Styrofoam raft, erect a shack on it, and drop an anchor a few yards from a very valuable shoreline. So far most of the legislative effort has been to little avail. Zoning laws start to get blurry once you extend them into the ocean. The trouble is no one really "owns" the ocean—sovereign states make treaties over it; nations fight on and under it, patrol it, take possession of the seabed below. But the water itself, and the things that float around on it, they tend to scoot away when the creaky pincer jaws of civilization attempt to snap shut.

The result of all this pressure and prejudice is that the "boat people" of the keys tend to be close-mouthed about their own. So it took most of the morning to confirm that the artist who lived aboard in the Coral Canal section of Stock Island was one Paula Davis and that her boat was called *Green Flash*. That's a popular name for a boat down here, on account of romantic and mystical notions about the strobelike band of color that sometimes appears at the horizon for an instant before the sun rises.

God's green flashbulb is what Mutt calls it. According to Mutt, seeing it brings luck. But there are those who say the eerie flash signals doom. I prefer Mutt's version. Then again, I've never seen it. At dawn it's all I can do to look for a coffeecup.

Scanning the narrow length of Coral Canal with binoculars, I located the houseboat. A shedlike affair built on an old work barge. Shingled haphazardly. Flat roof covered with asphalt. You could see where recent repairs had been made to the roof. Someone had taken the trouble to paint the shed door and what little trim there was. There were a few port-holes, different sizes, and a shuttered window. Typical ark in paradise. A lone pelican stood sentinel on the roof.

Getting to it was not easy. The canal had been chewed through the limestone base by heavy equipment some years before, as the first stage of a housing development. The development had never happened and the banks of the canal had been overgrown with the mangroves and the puckerbrush that creep back in as soon as men give up on anything down here. There were decaying concrete abutments softening like chalk in the sun. Moldy foundations for dream houses. Skeletal iron re-rod poking up through the undergrowth. Puddles of dead water that didn't appear until you put your foot down.

As I worked my way down to the steep bank of the canal, I heard little animal skitterings. Ground birds, I hoped, or lizards. I have nothing against snakes, so long as they don't attempt to occupy my immediate vicinity. Most anything sounds like a snake if you can't see it. Smart people wear leather boots when mucking through swampy, overgrown landscape. I was wearing sneakers; therefore, I wasn't smart. Therefore, I deserved to get bitten by a mangrove viper. The experts will tell you there is no such thing as a mangrove viper. Well, they haven't heard the invisible slithering when they're wearing only sneakers and gym socks. The experts who doubt the existence of the mangrove viper are the same boys who missed the coelacanth and the walking catfish.

What with the vipers and the walking catfish, I was in an altered state by the time I found the skiff tied up to the edge of the canal. I climbed in it immediately because it is well-known that mangrove vipers will not board a skiff in daylight. There was an oar under the seat and I took that up just in case there was one nearby who didn't know the rules.

After a little while my heart stopped trying to find a way out of my chest. When I trusted my voice I stood up and shouted.

"Ahoy, *Green Flash*! Anybody home?"

The words came back at me from a couple of different directions. The pelican looked pissed off as it took to wing. The houseboat was anchored in midcanal, thirty yards from either shore. The water was motionless, mirror-still. The floating shed looked lived in, but I'd known as soon as I located the skiff there was no one home. If Paula Davis had been aboard, the skiff would have been tied up to the houseboat. It wasn't; therefore, she wasn't. I was hailing just for the pleasure of hearing my own voice, and to scare away any slithery wildlife.

After a little careful reconnoitering I found what I'd been hoping to find: a path hacked through the undergrowth. You could see where a machete had slashed at the mangrove roots. Fresh cuts. It would be a constant effort, keeping the path clear. Thankful for Paula Davis' diligence, I followed the path back to the stretch of broken-up asphalt that had been the original development access. The heat was stunning. I was wearing a long-billed cap and shades and still the light found a way to numb my eyes. Never mind, I kept right to the asphalt, letting it grip at the treads of my sneakers. One snake-infested jungle interlude per day, that was my maximum.

With the heat and the light I didn't see my coupe until I was almost on it. At first glance it appeared to have sunk into the road. Then I saw that all four tires were flat. My trusty conch cruiser is not immune to flats, but it hardly ever gets more than two at once. And the windshield looked remarkably clean. Too clean. It wasn't there anymore. It had been shattered into a million crystal fragments. I looked in through the opening. Broken glass everywhere. The seats had been slashed. Viciously. The tires gaped like black wounds.

Right about then I heard something crashing through the mangroves. Something large. I dropped to the ground and hugged the burning asphalt. Whatever it was, it was coming my way. Fast.

4

THE beast was a mongrel, and friendly, from the sound of its tail thumping against the fender. All I could see of it was four yellow paws and a black nose sniffing at me under the sagging Cadillac. Probably wondering why a grown man would squeeze himself under an automobile at the mere sound of canine thrashing in the underbrush. I was wondering that myself. Decided it was the dread idea of mangrove vipers that had me spooked. That and the sight of my old cruiser sliced to ribbons.

"Woof woof," the dog said.

Woof woof also happened to be the sound I made trying to work myself out from under the car. The chassis seemed to be seeking a lower level as the last puffs of air escaped from the slashed tires. So it was woof, and then a little backward action, using my hands as flippers. The indignity. I knew how a walrus must feel, working backward off a hot gravel beach.

Meantime the yellow dog started licking my ankles. Under the right conditions getting your ankles licked can be interesting. Not while being crushed by a couple of tons of Detroit iron. During the final heave backward the Caddy bit a little chunk out of my left ear. Woozily I sat up. The dog transferred his attention to the blood and sweat dripping from my earlobe.

I growled. The animal whined and panted. Swampy dog breath.

"Beat it, Rover. Vamoose."

Someone had tied a red bandanna around the dog's neck. Not likely to be a stray, then. A bandanna on a pet was the kind of cute gesture that might be construed as artistic. Houseboat Paula was an artist; therefore, it was reasonable to assume the dog belonged to her. I looked for a collar, an ID tag. No dice.

"Tell the boss T. D. Stash requests an audience."

The dog said, "Woof!"

Getting new tires on the coupe killed the afternoon. While a Stock Island mechanic fitted retreads, I vacuumed out the broken glass and covered the shredded vinyl upholstery with duct tape. About a mile of it. Whoever had done the carving had used a very sharp instrument. Razor knife, maybe, or a honed switchblade. The cuts were straight, deep, evenly spaced, like claw marks. Workmanlike, in a nasty way.

I had no ready answer to the obvious question of who done it. A random act of vandalism? Or had the Caddy been a stand-in for me? I could think of a few Stock Island residents who had no excess of affection for me, but none who would be likely to take it out on an inanimate object. Slashing throats is considered machismo in the Cuban enclave, slashing up a Cadillac, even an old one, borders on the sacrilegious. So scratch any of my waterfront rivals. Paula Davis protecting her turf? A possibility, although the chauvinist in me preferred to think the blade wielder was male, with a powerful wrist and forearm. Which would leave out Graham Chilly, unless he'd put on weight and strength since his graduation picture was snapped.

The mechanic, a tough little Cuban with anthracite

eyes, never asked who had performed the surgery. What he did do was offer me a shot of espresso with the carefully itemized bill. I tossed down the bitter-sweet coffee, glad of the quick caffeine lift, and dropped the little paper cup in the wastebasket.

"The windshield, he's a problem. I call around, but nobody got. Maybe Marathon. Maybe Miami."

Maybe Miami. That's the ready answer in the Lower Keys. It means mañana, or possibly never.

Driving back into Key West, I decided the lack of windshield was an improvement. Plenty of air, perfect visibility, except where the bugs smacked up against my sunglasses. And miracle of miracles, the tape deck was still functioning. I slipped in *Chuck Berry's Golden Hits* and fast-forwarded to "Havana Moon."

Roll over Beethoven, and tell Fidel the news.

Top down, glass out, and blasting fat rock licks that echoed off the gingerbread houses of Eaton Street, I was the height of cool—for a lazy conch wharf rat. Maybe that explained the shivers in my spine.

I decided to postpone my visit to the Palmetto Key Time-Share Resort, where the late-afternoon hypno-tour of prospects would be under way. There were a couple of questions I wanted Mrs. Chilly to answer and it would be better to confront her alone, with plenty of daylight around us. Meantime I would make the rounds, see if her son had been sighted at any of the locals.

First stop was the counter at El Cacique, on the north end of Duval, where they know how to prepare a heaping plate of yellow rice, black beans, and the best picadillo north of Cuba. When my belt felt comfortably tight, I showed Graham's picture to Rosie. She wiped her hands on the towel tucked in the waist of her jeans, squinted at the snapshot, and said, "Cute kid. You hittin' on boys now, T.D.?"

"Graham is late for dinner. His mommy misses him."

"Well . . ." Rosie shrugged, pursing lips blurred with tangerine gloss. Her small breasts quivered against her thin cotton T-shirt. The café's logo, an Indian chief, was emblazoned on the shirt. I couldn't help noticing that her left nipple made a cleft in his chin.

"He ain't had dinner in here," she said, watching me check out the chief. "Not tonight and not lately."

"But you know him?"

"Not by name. Just that he looks familiar. Could be with the wise-ass gang that hangs across the street." She jerked her thumb at the plate-glass window, where the sign for Rick's Café was visible in the jumble of Duval Street.

"Thanks, Rosie."

"I see him, you want I should say something?"

"Yeah. Tell him to go home for supper."

Rick's is an upstairs/downstairs saloon, wide open to the street. There was a lull in business and the bar was actually visible—usually it is obscured by layers of tanned young flesh, plastic cups of draft beer, and gaggy shots of gumdrop-flavored schnapps. Lenny, one of the young bar managers, handed me a cold bottle of ale and chuckled when he looked at the snap of Graham.

"Son of Kong," he said. "Godzilla Junior. He's the brat with the old man does that crummy Elvis impersonation."

"Not to mention Johnny Cash and Conway Twitty."

"Yeah, well, the little dweeb came in here once, insisted I put one of the old guy's cassettes on the machine, right? I tell him, I go, take it up with the DJ. The DJ tells him to get lost, next thing I know the kid is asking him to step outside. So I go over, try to straighten him out, he decides he wants *me* to step outside. Matter of honor, he says." The big bartender grinned at the thought. A Southern Californian by birth and disposition, Lenny had a hot thing going with a Nautilus machine, and looked it. "Stash, I tell you the little shit's not breaking a hundred pounds, right? But he's ready to take on the world. So what I did, I tucked the cassette in his shirt pocket and then I tucked him in that trash basket at the curb. Feet first. Not wanting to totally humiliate the kid. Thing was, I kind of admired his courage."

"He ever come back?"

"Not inside here. Out on the sidewalk, at the stand-up bar."

"When?"

"Must have been a week back. I only remember because I look out there and he's giving me the thumbs-up. Which surprised me. I figured he did anything, he'd give me the finger."

"Was he alone?"

"Hard to say. My impression, he was with some kids, locals. The thumbs-up was to impress them he was tight with me. Not that I remember it real clear. One shift is like another from back here."

And one young face was like another, as I confirmed at a dozen saloons in a three-block radius. Graham looked familiar. He might have been in recently. With the quantity of beer-drenched college kids and sun-drenched yahoos and grizzly-eyed shrimpers pouring through town, Charlie Manson could have been in recently and not left a lasting impression.

There was a harsh, hot wind sweeping in from the northeast. On Duval Street all the drunks seemed to be leaning in the same direction, like giddy sailboats bending to the breeze. I found myself leaning with them, trudging from bar to bar. Flashing the picture to anyone who would take a look.

I crashed a gay disco on Angela Street, figuring maybe Graham Chilly waltzed both ways. The willowy bartender said he'd never seen him.

"This looks like jailbait, mister," he smirked, handing the photograph back. "Is that really what you want?"

"What I want is a Cruzan rum, straight up," I said to the smirk. "In a glass, not a plastic cup. This here's my kid brother. You sure he ain't been around here?"

My mother, God rest her, taught me better than to say "ain't," but after the third drink I tend to forget. I left the rum there in the glass when a slab of beef in pink shades started calling me sailor.

Looking for Graham was a dirty job, but somebody had to do it. I tacked upwind into a Cuban grocery and downed a double espresso. That helped. There was a bleached-blond señora behind the counter. Without meeting my eyes she took the picture, then banged the palm of her hand against the thin partition at the rear of the store. Her husband appeared, wiping his hands on a paper towel. He glanced at Graham and shook his head.

"Go away, please," he said. "Very busy tonight."

"I'm the only one in the store. You call that busy?"

"Go away please."

His hand went beneath the counter. Before it came up again I was back on the street. In Key West your average Cuban grocer has more firepower than a SWAT team. To argue with such a man in his place of business is to risk sudden, high-caliber ventilation. Contemplating their overreaction to a mere photograph, I started cutting north, through quiet residential neighborhoods, toward the docks at Land's End.

Somewhere on William Street a Maxi Taxi pulled up to the curb.

"Need a lift, handsome?"

The voice from inside the van sounded familiar. I leaned against the open window on the passenger side. A lighter clicked, illuminating her face.

"Trudy? I'm only going about five blocks."

"Destination?"

I told her.

"Get in, you big lunk. I'm going off-duty."

Near as I could tell, Trudy inhaled for all five blocks. At Land's End she cut through the dirt parking lots to the commercial dock area and parked the taxi van opposite Zach's Bar. The wind was still strong from Florida Bay, redolent of salt and baitfish and the dead stink of mangrove. I declined the offer of a hit. For me, rum and sensi don't mix.

"Been one of those days, Stash." Trudy sighed, then licked her fingers and extinguished the number. "I figure, what the hell, might as well be one of those nights."

I followed her into Zach's, watching her sun-streaked ponytail bounce against her bare brown shoulders. Her long, shapely legs extruded from loose cotton shorts cut high enough so you could, if you tried, catch just a glimpse of cheek.

"What are you doing"—Trudy laughed—"bent over like that?"

"Dropped my lucky penny."

"Uh huh."

At the bar Trudy ordered a bottle of beer and plunked it against my thimble of rum.

"If I remember correctly, you were supposed to meet me at Smathers Beach. Two months ago."

"I'm running late," I said. "Are you mad?"

"I got over it."

Zachary C. Malone's waterfront saloon was a hangout for his fishing and smuggling cronies, who kept boats within stumbling distance. A lot of other locals went there who liked to pretend they were fishermen or smugglers. This in turn attracted tourists, the ones brave enough to range beyond Duval Street. The result was a liquor trade that kept two cash registers and four bartenders busy. Most of the bartenders were related to Malone and looked it. Wiry red hair, thick necks, pale-green eyes, and small white teeth.

"Zach around?" I asked one of the young Malone clones.

He shrugged, looking me over. "Not tonight," he said after a while, then turned his back. It was a big back, well-muscled. A trap fisherman's back. I was returning the school photograph to my shirt pocket when Trudy placed her slim hand over mine.

"That's Graham Chilly," she said, squinting.

"Know him?"

"Sure. Kept me busy one night, driving him all over the island. Tipped me a hundred bucks. A high-school kid with deep pockets."

"When was this?"

"Couple weeks back. I could check my log books, you need to know."

I considered it, then shrugged. "Maybe later, he doesn't turn up soon. So tell me, Trudy, what's he like?"

Trudy was drinking the beer. The muscles in her slender throat bobbed as she swallowed. Her eyes smiled at me over the edge of the bottle. Flecks of electric blue under long lashes. I wondered why I hadn't kept that date at Smathers Beach.

"The kid?" Trudy said, patting her lips with the back of her hand. "I thought he was pretty funny."

"Ha-ha funny or weird funny?"

"Little of each. I laugh easy and he got a kick out

of that. 'Course you drive a cab on this island, you better learn to laugh at dumb jokes, and his jokes weren't any dumber than most, I reckon."

"I reckon?"

She grinned. "I grew up in Lincoln, Nebraska. We used to say things like 'I reckon' and 'Howdy, stranger.' "

"Sure grow 'em purty out on the pray-ree."

"You talkin' about me?"

"I thought I was. I've never been to Nebraska. So tell me, what was Graham doing, having you drive him all over the island?"

For some reason that took a lot of the smile out of her face. She stared at the bottle in her hand, considering the question. I was beginning to regret asking it when she said, "He was delivering gifts. Or that's what he told me. Had five or six of these little gift-wrapped boxes, about the size you'd put cuff links in, or earrings."

"So what was it," I said. "Cuff links, or earrings?"

"I told you the kid gave me a hundred-dollar tip. Also he gave me one of the little boxes. I get home and open it up and it's a deck of cocaine. Ten grams."

Which made it more like an eleven-hundred-dollar tip. Not bad for an evening behind the wheel.

"Sounds, Trudy, like you were an accessory to a crime."

She nodded, keeping her voice low as she confided, "Man, I was freaked. I mean, it never occurred to me, he was making *those* kinds of deliveries. Not all done up in little boxes with little blue ribbons. Honest, T.D., the last thing I need is to get busted for chauffeuring a dealer. You know how the law works in this state—you get two years for transporting twenty tons of marijuana, but get caught selling an ounce of coke and you'll still be in Raiford when the millennium arrives."

Two young shrimpers were arm-wrestling at the other end of the bar, attracting a crowd. The one with the fuzzy yellow mustache closed his eyes, his jaw muscles twitching as he attempted to put down pin his opponent's wrist. The opponent looked to be another of the Malone clan. When he eventually won, there was a roar of approval. Plastic cups appeared at my elbow, turned bottom up. A round on the house.

"Step outside?" I said to Trudy. "I need a breath of air."

Trudy smiled, hooking a hand in the waist of my jeans as we cut through the crowd and found the side door. The heavy planked dock sagged away from the rear of Zach's Bar. The wind was backing to the east, finally, as the tide turned, and the air smelled salty fresh. Out on the pier a white net boat was backed under the chute, taking on a load of ice.

Trudy's lithe body pressed against me. We kissed briefly, but I was distracted by the white boat and the crew attending it.

"Hang on," I said, slipping away. "I have to see Malone."

"I'll have a smoke," she said, irritated. "Then I'm going back inside."

The new boat with the shiny white hull was a recent addition to Zach Malone's fleet. A couple of his boys were in the stern, going over the gill nets. They ignored me as I came into the floodlights from the icehouse.

"Zach around?"

I had to shout to make myself heard above the generator. The pair tending the nets exchanged glances, then shook their heads in tandem. They'd have made a nice tag team. There was a redhead standing at the deck hatch, guiding the ice chute. He shouted something toward the wheelhouse when I jumped from the pier to the boat. The generator cut out abruptly.

"We're busy, mister. This here's a private vessel."

"Just want to see Zach Malone. Won't take but a minute." I started to reach into my back pocket for the photograph of Graham. A hand grabbed my wrist. I turned and found myself pinned against the hatch cover, held down by the two goons who'd been messing with the nets.

"Anybody know this dude?"

"He looks like the one runs that guide boat out of Mutt's dock."

The other goon squinted at me, nodding as the information penetrated. He got a sly look. "Tarpon are running tonight, mister. How come you ain't working?"

I expressed my delight at hearing that the tarpon were gallivanting in the moonlight and explained that what I really wanted was to see Zach Malone, if they would be so good as to announce me. The kid holding the ice chute laughed. He was a teenager with a raw, rangy build and the small, palm-green eyes that ran in the family.

"This dude's got a mouth on him, huh?"

He stepped down from the edge of the hatch and picked up the aluminum shovel he'd been using to sluice the ice down the chute. The two goons let me up. I massaged my wrists, forcing the blood back into my hands.

"Why the rough stuff? I have a couple of questions for the boss, that's all."

"Maybe," said the kid with the shovel, "we don't like questions."

"Tell you what," I said. "Let's go into the wheelhouse and try asking Zach."

"Zach ain't in there."

He was, though. I could see his silhouette behind

the smoked plexiglass as he watched his boys man-
handle an intruder.

The two goons tried to block my way. I butted
through, knocking one of them down, and got about
three steps closer to Zach Malone before the shovel
slammed into the side of my head.

5

I woke up on the floor. Well, not the floor exactly, but on the kind of anemic bedroll called a futon. Various sensations confirmed there was a slender body curled against me. I summoned the courage to crack open one eye. Trudy.

Well, now.

Right about then a bongo drum went off in the left side of my head. Pernicious rhythm orchestrated by an overdose of rum and single shot of shovel. I remembered small green eyes, a row of teeth as soft and white as Chiclets: a species of Malone, looming down over me. Someone saying, "I cracked him good, Pa," followed by hollow laughter. A sensation of flying through darkness and then . . .

Trudy to the rescue? I lay there with her long limbs curled over mine, trying to put it all together. Cracked upside the skull, followed by a three-count heave-ho that landed me not in the water, as I'd feared, but on the ice-house dock. The surly, guttural noise of the diesels revving—that had been Malone's net boat pulling away from the wharf. The splash that brought me back, and that my first groggy instincts assumed was the prologue to drowning, was Trudy pouring a cup of beer in my face.

"Bud Light," she apologized. "It was the best I could do. What'd you say to those guys, made 'em whack you like that?"

After that the evening went a little hazy. There was a long, staggering walk back to Trudy's little Palm Avenue apartment. Some kissy face on her front steps. And if I wasn't imagining things, an interlude of lovemaking on the aforementioned futon.

I went to brush the hair from Trudy's eyes and found them open.

"If you're wondering," she said, her voice silky with sleep, "yes, we did."

"I remember everything."

"I doubt it. You kept passing out. Or falling asleep. I got an idea, though," she said, reaching for me, "how to refresh your memory."

It was near on noon by the time I finished my second cup of coffee. The bruise on my cheekbone throbbed when I smiled. You have to smile when a beautiful, long-legged woman sits opposite you in a scoop-neck T-shirt and translucent panties. As she spooned at a honeydew melon, Trudy kept flashing a grin right back at me.

"See what you missed, you stood me up at Smathers Beach?"

"I am but a poor fool," I said. "Bruised and battered."

"You got a blue circle under your eye," she said, pointing with the spoon. "Reminds me of Arthur Godfrey. Those tea-bag pouches."

"You're not old enough to remember Arthur Godfrey."

"In Nebraska I was old enough. Takes a long time for the broadcast to get to Nebraska."

"I reckon it does."

"So," Trudy said, pushing the melon rind away. "You figure Graham Chilly is in big trouble?"

"Big enough. If he managed to get himself crossed up with the Malones, they'll dice him up for chum. Unless I can get to him first."

When I left, Trudy was painting her toenails a phosphorescent orange.

"I hope you're not too late," she sighed, huffing air at her shapely feet. "Kids like Graham, they just get et up, you know? Someone bigger and stronger and hungrier comes along and just decides to chow down on 'em."

Outside, the palm fronds were being rustled by a hot noon wind that stunk of sulfur from the power plant. I borrowed Trudy's bicycle and peddled back to my place, thinking about baitfish, and sharks with eyes as green as money.

The tour trolley was just leaving as I steered the coupe through the hot pink gates of the Palmetto Key Time-Share Resort. There was a big four-color billboard of Famous Floyd right where the blacktop ended and the limestone marl dust began. Floyd with one arm slung over a guitar, the other gesturing at an artist's rendering of what the condo towers would look like when they were finished. Which, from the evidence, was a long way off.

The dust was being spewed up by a trenching machine. The operator stood behind it, shaded by a palm-frond sombrero as the giant, chainsawlike device chewed slowly through the fossilized base of the island. At the rate he was going, the excavation work would proceed only slightly faster than natural erosion. The billboard showed six round condominium towers on stilts over a lush, tropical landscape. Stucco wedding cakes on a sea of lime sherbert. What met the eye was one ten-story tower, more or less complete, two more in early stages of construction, and one shallow pit filled with brackish water. A cow bird teetered by the water's edge, flexing dirty white wings.

I parked the coupe off to one side and followed

the signs. The reception center was in the shaded area under the completed building. Hanging plants dripped down from the curved concrete stilts, creating a sort of store-bought oasis in a hot and dusty moonscape. The sales team, having just seen off a load of the bused-in prospects who had agreed to endure the spiel in exchange for complimentary gift packages, had collapsed in canvas chairs near the little phony tiki bar. One of them got wearily to his feet and headed me off.

"Welcome to Palmetto Key, a time-share resort," he said, wiping his mouth with the back of his hand. "Next introductory tour is in twenty minutes. Can I get y'all something cool to drink?"

"Sarsaparilla. Straight up."

"Huh? What we got is wine coolers, mostly."

"You look good in that pink flowered shirt, Dave. I notice that isn't your name on the pocket. Must have got mixed up in the laundry, huh?"

Dave squinted. "Stash? That you? Shit, man, them wraparound Ray-Bans cover half your face. What y'all doin' sneakin' up on me here?"

"I'm in the market for a few dozen time slots, Dave ol' buddy. Fix me up?"

"Hey, y'all can have your pick. No money down, easy payments."

"Close any deals lately?" I said.

"Gimme a break, bubba," he said, leaning back against a concrete underpinning, hooking his thumbs in the generous waist of his chino slacks. "I got me three more days. Then I collect my draw, run like hell to cash it while the check's still good, and haul my sorry ass out of here. Next week you want to find Dave Starky, check the Boca Chica Bar."

"That bad?"

"Look around, man. The brochures look slick, but the, ah, reality of the situation tends to discourage the suckers." He grinned. "I mean the prospects. Hey, y'all still drivin' that big ragtop Coupe de Ville I sold ya?"

"Yeah, and I'm looking for a chauffeur. You want to apply?"

"I'm gonna head me on up to Marathon. They moving serious real estate up that way. Real waterfront stuff, oceanside, none of this canal-front bullshit."

"I thought you were going to the Boca Chica?"

"Right," he said. "That's where I'm takin' my vacation. Second stool from the back wall. Got my eye on a little Cuban girl in there, likes to lap dance after hours."

"Reggie around?"

"Who? Aw, you mean Her Highness, Queen Regina," he drawled, rhyming it with vagina. "Yeah, she's in the barn."

"The what?"

"What we call the place you take a prospect to close the sale. What it is is her office. Right up them steps."

I started toward a spiral of concrete steps.

"Say, bubba," Dave said, catching my arm. "There something I should know? One of your lawyer friends send you over to collect paper? Maybe shut this place down?"

"Nothing like that."

A cloud of marl dust approached. The next trolley full of prospects, all of them clutching complimentary gift chits. Dave sighed and hitched up his belt. I went up the spiral, into the air-conditioned atmosphere of the condominium tower.

Discernible over the sigh of the air-exchange unit was the plunk of a guitar and a rough baritone voice. Johnny Cash singing "Ring of Fire." After a bar or so my ears told me it was not Cash, but a credible impersonation by Floyd Chilly. The tune went down, down, down, while I went up.

The first thing you noticed, as you came into the carpeted foyer, was the wall of windows. Then you realized the windows were really rear projection screens, part of a cleverly orchestrated illusion. Bright, color-saturated transparencies of Mallory Dock, a palm grove at Smathers Beach, a windsurfer kicking up a glistening spray. The screens switched images every eight or ten seconds. Splashy snapshots of bikinied bodies, leaping fish, lingering sunsets: a dream sequence of life in the Lower Keys.

I knew then why the "barn" was inside, why likely prospects were herded up here for the closing. Away from the unpleasant distraction of dust and noise, the stink of construction. Away from reality. Stick with the illusion of pleasure, kids, and sign on the dotted line.

Regina Chilly had her back to me. She was standing up, speaking into a telephone that had been fitted with a privacy mouth guard. Dressed for success in a raw-linen jacket, matching pleated skirt, severly high heels, and a tangerine silk scarf. If the tension evident in her slim shoulders was any indication, the conversation wasn't a happy one. When she slammed the phone down and said, "Son of a goddamn bitch!" the conjecture was confirmed.

"Sign me up for a couple of units," I said. "Maybe that will improve your mood."

Mrs. Chilly didn't like being surprised. The slate-gray eyes contracted to slits. Her lips, glossed to match the tangerine scarf, tightened into an unpleasant pout. You had to be quick to see it, because within a heartbeat the official welcoming smile was back and the mascara-thickened lashes were fluttering.

"I didn't hear you come in," she said sweetly.

"There's a little bar over there next to the model, help yourself. I'll be with you in just a moment."

"I'm not here for the pitch, Mrs. Chilly."

The smile froze. "Oh?"

"T. D. Stash," I said. "Your husband hired me to track down Graham."

"Oh."

"You remember Graham," I said. "Skinny kid with big ideas. Until recently he was residing at your domicile. Your son the coke pusher. Am I ringing any bells?"

Regina Chilly put her hips through a hydraulic pivot and marched toward an open office door, indicating that I follow.

"Don't get shirty," she instructed. "And watch your mouth."

"Yes, ma'am."

I wasn't sure what "getting shirty" meant, but I knew how to watch my mouth. She eased the door shut and gestured at a chair. I dropped into it while she sat on the edge of a desk, running a pencil through her fingers like a miniature baton. Staring me down. The kind of power stare they teach in assertiveness training.

I met her eyes for a count of twenty, then put my hands over my face and whimpered. "You win, Mrs. Chilly. Another ten seconds and I'd be rolling belly up and barking like a dog."

The shades in the small office were drawn, so you couldn't see the condos that weren't built yet.

"What do you want?"

"I want to find your son."

She nodded, drumming the eraser end of the pencil against the desktop. "And you're doing so," she said, lashing me with her crisply correct enunciation, "out of the kindness of your heart."

"Floyd and I have an arrangement."

"How nice for you. Tell me, is it absolutely necessary you wear those ridiculous sun goggles inside?"

"Absolutely," I said, and made a show of twid-
dling my thumbs.

"If my husband wrote you a check, be warned
that unless countersigned by me it will, as you Yanks
say, bounce."

"Couple of things wrong with that, Mrs. Chilly.
First, since this island is as far south as you can get
and still be in the United States of America, and
since I was born here, I hardly qualify as a Yank. A
Yankee is someone from about a thousand miles
north of here. Second, your husband didn't write
me any checks—we have a gentleman's agreement: I
find Graham and get him out of whatever trouble
he's surely headed for and Floyd will give me that
fishing machine he's got, The *Golden Oldie*. And last
and most assuredly not least, my information is that
even those checks graced with your signature are
likely to, as you Brits say, fuck a duck."

Regina laughed. As she uncrossed her ankles her
nylons made a little zinging sound that ran up my
spine. "Fuck a duck?" she said.

"Off the top of my head, ma'am. I was searching
for an appropriate phrase and that one intruded
itself. Was that shirty of me?"

"More dirty. Also," she said, appearing to relax,
"somewhat amusing. Would you do me a favor?
Don't call me 'ma'am'. It makes me feel like a
grandmother."

"Regina?"

"Reggie. Regina is, as Floyd says, a tight-ass name,
and I am trying very hard not to be a tight-ass sort of
person. As you just witnessed, I sometimes fail. You
caught me after a most distressing phone call and
I'm afraid we got off on the wrong foot. Can we start
over?"

"Sure," I said. "You want me to go out the door, come in again? Then you can say, 'Have you found my son? I've been worried sick.' And I can say, 'No, I haven't found him. Do you mind answering a few questions that might make my job easier?' And you say 'I'll do anything to help.' "

Reggie stood up, slipping one hand into her jacket pocket. She tapped the pencil lightly against her chin and said thoughtfully, "We're getting off on the wrong foot again. Why is that?"

"I've got a theory," I said. "My theory is that you don't want me looking for Graham. You're not even pretending to act like a worried mom, and that worries me. You don't want me finding the kid, and *that* worries me."

"Stop worrying, Mr. T. D. Stash. Graham is just fine."

"When's the last time you talked to him."

"Oh," she said, smiling secretly as she glanced at her watch. "I'd say it was about ten minutes ago."

"That was Graham on the phone?"

"None other," she said, pivoting toward the shaded window. Knife cuts of light wrapped her thin figure. "As I assumed, he's run off with a girl."

"This girl has a name?"

"He didn't say," she said, keeping her face averted.

"Just a minute ago you said the phone call was distressing, upsetting."

When she turned back, her eyes were leveled at me. "I don't see why I should discuss my son with you. He's my flesh and blood and I'll worry about him in my own way."

"I don't know about the girl without a name, Mrs. Chilly, but I know a few other things. Graham is paddling up a dangerous creek. He gets in too far, I won't be able to get him out." I stood up. Even with the steep heels, Regina Chilly was barely shoulder-high to me. "If you have any influence with the boy, tell him to give it up. Tell him to come home."

I lifted the sunglasses and showed her the puffed eye, the bruise on my cheek. "This was just a love tap. They go after Graham, it won't be with fists."

In the foyer the slide show continued to flash seductive images of paradise. Famous Floyd Chilly was singing a song made famous by someone else. As I opened the door to the stairwell a phone began to chirp; a pair of heels tick-tocked purposefully across the carpet.

Under the condo tower the heat was waiting, as sneaky as a process server. Dave Starky and his sales team had corralled the prospects in the phony little tiki bar. I could hear a blender screaming and the names of tropical drinks being chanted like an invocation.

6

Lily agreed to meet me at the Laughing Gull. I sat at the bar at the end of the wharf, playing with the ice in my iced tea and thinking about mothers. Mothers who didn't ask the right questions or give the right answers. Mothers who looked the other way when their sons retailed narcotics. Mothers whose nylons went zing.

My lawyer friend was a half-hour late. I bought a cigar, stared at it. The trades were driving in from the southeast, stirring up a ragged chop in the basin. The swells banged against the pilings, giving a subtle sea motion to the wharf. The cocktail napkins were nailed down with smooth beach stones and the bartender was urging the customers to keep their glasses topped off, lest they blow away.

"You better give me a bottle of beer," I said. "I feel light-headed."

"It's the wind," he said, snapping off the cap. "Dries you out. I move down here from Jersey, it's just like in the pictures. Except for the wind. You can't feel that blowing, you look at the pictures."

"Good sailing weather," I said. "Bad fishing."

Lily waltzed in, sleek and satisfied. Sam was with her, wearing a white one-piece swimsuit, a pair of running shorts, and a deep tan.

"I can see why you're late," I said, carrying my beer over to a table as the two women dropped into canvas deck chairs. "You were having a nap, as the saying goes."

Sam pushed a glossy black bang from her forehead and smiled. "You ought to be a detective," she said. "Or maybe a Peeping Tom. What's wrong with your face?"

"Ran into a doorknob."

"So you are a Peeping Tom."

"I are if you say I are."

"He's a fishing guide," Lily said, scanning the menu.

"Is that like a Michelin guide?"

"Worse," she said. "He's not rated. When he's not showing snowbirds how to land tarpon, which is most of the time, he's bumping into doorknobs named Malone."

"You heard about that, huh?"

"This is a very small island, T.D." Lily let go of the paper menu. It flew out over the water like a thin green bird.

"Just order the conch fritters," I said. "You can't go wrong."

"What I'm going to do, I'm going to tell you to be careful."

"And I'm going to say, fine, help me be careful by telling me what's the lowdown on the Palmetto Key Time-Share Resort."

Lily stared at me and shook her head. "Client privilege. I represent the Chillys in certain delicate negotiations."

"You set me up for the job, Lil. Theoretically I'm doing legwork for you."

"The resort is a separate issue."

A waitress wandered out from the restaurant to the bar. Sam ordered the fritters and a salad and watched the waitress walk away. Lily watched her watching the waitress and then gave me a weak little smile. She had a history of falling in love with faithless girlfriends. It was something we had in common.

"Fine," I said. "I'm going to take a big fat guess and say the place is about to go Chapter Eleven. But I don't really care about the details, I just need to know what the Chillys stand to lose personally if the resort goes down the tubes."

"Tell me why it's pertinent to locating Graham."

I explained that Floyd thought the boy was trying to raise money for the family by putting together a drug deal of some kind.

"Is that what you think is happening?"

"It's a possibility. Mommie dearest claims she's been in contact with the kid, so he isn't exactly missing. On the other hand his stepdad still wants him brought home, before he does something that could earn him the kind of time that's not for sale even at Palmetto Key Resort."

Lily nodded and thought about it. I sipped at my beer and talked sailboats with Sammie, who ran the windsurfer concession at the public beach. She competed professionally at sailboard regattas and had the shoulders and forearms to prove it. When the conch fritters were delivered, I was happy to see that her eyes no longer followed the waitress.

"What happened," Lily said, fiddling with her salad, "is that a bank in Kentucky went belly up. Said bank had been heavily invested in a Bahamian mutual fund that turned out to be a shell."

"Pardon me?"

"A phony corporation. Never mind, it's beside the point. What matters is that the bank went out of business, and when they went out of business they were no longer able to underwrite the Palmetto Key project. So the Chillys are scrambling. It takes a while to find another investment banker and meantime they have to keep the project afloat. So, yes, they are experiencing cash-flow problems. But I don't see how a high-school kid dealing grams to his friends could make the kind of money that would help."

"Floyd told you about that?"

"He likes to put on that folksy good-old-boy facade, but Floyd Chilly is no dummy. He knows Graham has been chipping and he knows the kid has more spending money than he should have. So he put two and two together. But two and two don't make a million, and that's what Palmetto Key needs in the short term, to keep construction ongoing."

Sam was stunting with the conch fritters, trying to throw one of the little dough balls up in the air and catch it in her mouth. The wind was throwing her timing off. Lily smiled indulgently and brushed the fritter from her lap.

"The problem I'm having," I said, "I'm caught in the middle. Dad wants me to find the prodigal stepson, and Mom gives me some load of cod's wallop about how he's run off with a girl, I should leave well enough alone."

"Maybe he has. Run off with a girl."

"If he has, it could be she's part of the deal he's trying to put together."

"How can you be sure he's doing that? Putting together a deal?"

I lifted the sunglasses.

"Right," Lily said. "A message from Zach Malone."

Sammie flipped the last fritter a little too high and a laughing gull swooped in, snatching it in midair.

"I'd like to be there," Sam said. "When the freakin' bird tries to explain why it has garlic on its breath."

Mutt was asleep with his eyes open. Hanging

from his slack mouth was the butt of a cigar. In his right hand, fingers curled instinctively tight, was a paper cup of rum. I noticed the cigar ash running down his T-shirt and wondered how close he had come to spontaneous combustion. It was unsettling, being stared at by an unconscious man, so I left him undisturbed and went out to the dock and gassed up *Bushwhacked*, my eighteen-footer.

The engine hadn't been fired in a week or so and took a while to catch. When I had the idle where it sounded sweet, I cast off the lines, flipped the bumpers inside the rail, and headed into the channel.

The chop was milky green in the basin. I turned southwest into it, with the idea of taking the short way around the island, a quick run on the Atlantic side. After the first few slams and dunks, I swung her through a 180 degrees and headed for the north cut around Fleming Key. The *Bushwhacked* was designed to glide through calm shallows—the flats— and putting her through a dry gale would be pure and unpleasant foolishness.

The run between the western banks and Fleming was relatively protected. *Bushwhacked* was able to get up on a plane and cruise at a steady fifteen knots without jarring my teeth loose. At that rate the Stock Island run would take less than an hour, which would leave me plenty of daylight to find Coral Canal and the *Green Flash*. I had it in mind to see if there was any truth to the little tale Regina Chilly told about Graham shacking up with a girl. There was also the nagging question about who it was who had slashed up my poor defenseless, overweight Cadillac.

Turning southeast around the tip of the old munitions dump the navy had turned into an island, I saw one of the glass-bottomed tour boats anchored

in the lee of Garrison Bight. With seas breaking over
the reef, her captain had wisely opted for calmer
waters. Even so, I saw a couple of snowbirds hanging over the stern: "How was the boat ride, Muffy?"
"Barfo, dear, absolutely barfo."

I cut it wide around Sigsbee, likewise a navy creation, because I'd once holed a boat on the stub
pilings that lurked in the shallows there, and for
other, less easily defined reasons. Maybe because a
certain Lieutenant Staskowski, married all of six
months to Eveline Porter of Southard Street, dumped
his SBD dive bomber there and drowned, unconscious, in three feet of water. My mother shortened
Staskowski to Stash, which also happened to be the
old man's nickname. I say the old man. Already I'd
outlived the guy by seven years. As for Eveline
Porter Stash, her eternal residence is now a bleached
white crypt in the old city cemetery, three blocks
east of where she'd been born.

I'd worked myself into a fine morbid mood by the
time I raised the Stock Island channel. I shut down
the outboard after clearing the bridge. Letting her
drift, I fished through the under-seat locker and
found the expanded chart for Key West and environs. Spreading it across my knees, I discovered that
Coral Canal wasn't shown. No surprise, really, since
the canal had been cut in to feed a proposed development that never happened.

I had a rough idea of where it intersected with the
channel. I didn't know how rough until I'd been to
Cow Key and back three times, scraping the mangroves in a search for the canal opening. Why didn't
Ms. Paula Davis have the good sense to park her
barge in the main channel with the rest of the houseboats? Coral Canal, as I remembered it from shore,
was hardly an ideal spot for a landscape painter—

although Hieronymus Bosch might have enjoyed it, what with the mongrel dogs and the backwater snakes.

T. S. Stash, intrepid navigator, was about ready to give it up as a bad go when a sneaky mangrove branch hooked on the bow rail. I used a machete to cut loose and was slipping the blade back into the sheath when I noticed a stretch of open water, barely visible, through the screen of leaves.

Stanley must have felt as I did when he closed at last on Livingstone's trail. I went to work with the machete, hacking at the sea-toughened branches, clearing the recent growth that had blinded the canal entrance. In my enthusiasm I almost missed noticing that there were other cuts, recent ones, on the lower branches. As if someone had wanted to clear only enough for a very narrow vessel, say a dingy or a canoe.

I looked at the machete in my hand, remembering the long, straight cuts in the coupe upholstery. The way the thick cords of the tires had been severed. Yes, a machete might have done it, wielded by a wrist at least as strong as mine.

That gave me pause. I looked back over the expanse of the open channel. An osprey was circling over Cow Key. The fleet of houseboats tugged at their moorings, facing the wind out of the south. Nothing out of the ordinary. Nothing visible, anyhow.

No reason to get spooked, Stash old buddy. Just finish cutting through the overgrowth and go about your business. So I chopped at the damnably tough mangrove until my arm ached, then took a breather and chopped some more. When I finally quit, the opening was just wide enough to slip *Bushwhacked* through without scraping paint.

Coral Canal had been cut into the island as a slow

S-turn, a narrow, meandering canal that the original developers must have assumed would look more natural. After a decade of overgrowth it looked very natural indeed. There wasn't any coral, of course, just the marl limestone that is the base of most of the keys south of Marathon, but real-estate promoters tend to avoid overusing reality. People think of the keys, they think coral, so why disabuse potential investors?

The rotting concrete abutments of the abandoned housing project pushed up through the clinging vegetation like architectural footnotes to a lost civilization. A pelican, probably the same one, was perched on the bow of the *Green Flash*. I kept the outboard throttled low, easing closer. The barge listed slightly to starboard, I noticed. A rainwater cistern, possibly, or maybe just careless stowing. The pelican stayed where it was, regarding me with impassive eyes.

"Anybody home, Admiral?" I said to the bird.

Not even a blink to acknowledge me. Pelicans are hard to impress. If you're not a fish, or you haven't got webbed feet, they're not much interested.

The blue skiff, I noticed, was tied to the mangroves in about the same place where I'd first discovered it. There were oars in it this time, so someone had used it since my first visit. It occurred to me that if someone—Graham, say—wanted to hide out on the houseboat, he could swim out to it and leave the skiff ashore as a sort of camouflage.

I maneuvered alongside, grabbed a dock line, and stepped aboard. *Bushwhacked* skidded backward, jerking at the line in my hands. I wove the line over a rusty galvanized deck cleat, then thumped my fist against the cabin trunk.

"Come out, come out, whoever you are," I said, directing my voice at one of the curtained portholes. "Time's up, game's over."

The pelican squawked. I lost my footing, grabbed the edge of the roof, hauled myself back aboard. A very minor miscue, certainly no reason to start the heart pounding. What was it about this desolate little bayou that got me spooked so easy?

When my pulse returned to something like normal, I did a circumnavigation of the cabin, bending down to try to get a glimpse of the inside through the portholes. I could have ripped through one of the screens and pushed the curtains aside, but that would have been vandalism and I wasn't in the mood. The door, I discovered, was padlocked. A nice, case-hardened padlock. More than a match for a case-hardened, unlicensed retriever of missing persons. I pulled at the door, rattling it against the hasp. A gap showed between the door and the uneven jamb.

Crouching, I took off my Ray-Bans and worked my fingers into the gap. When I had it maxed out, I put my face to the slice of darkness and let my eyes adjust. At first I could pick out only vague shapes, illuminated by faint pools of light from the curtained portholes. Gradually the inside of the cabin began to make sense. A long, open passageway, running the length of the barge. A partial bulkhead that screened off a small area, possibly the galley. Normal household furniture: a sofa, chairs. A tilted worktable, the kind draftsmen use. Clothes hanging from a row of pegs—woman-type clothes.

Not exactly a drug runner's dream boat. And if Graham was in there somewhere he had the uncanny ability to blend in with inanimate objects.

"Yoo hoo," I said into the gap, just for the heck of it. "Can Graham come out and play?"

Something wet and hot splattered on the top of my head. Something else hit me, hard and sharp. I kept my fingers hooked in the door and spun around. The pelican looked down at me with one beady eye, poising its long bill for another jab. I swung my arm and it backed off, but not very far.

"Son of a bitch," I said, wiping the nasty little deposit from my hair. "Goddamn watchbird."

Don't let anyone tell you pelican shit doesn't burn. I finally had to duck my head into the stagnant canal, and came up feeling like I'd been dipped in slime. I had my eyes closed, so I heard Paula Davis before seeing her.

"I'm warning you," the voice said, close enough to give me a good jolt. "Leave Lautrec alone."

The vision before me, somewhat blurred, was of a slim, remarkably attractive young woman sitting in a blue skiff. She was holding an oar the way Wade Boggs holds a bat, like she was ready to hit one up the middle if I gave her the wrong pitch. She was wearing cutoff denim shorts, a pink tank top, and a green plastic visor that kept a mop of curly brown hair out of her eyes.

"Who's Lautrec?" I asked, attempting, without much luck, to dry myself on my damp shirtfront.

"Toulouse-Lautrec," she said. "The pelican."

"Are you Paula Davis, the artist?"

The oar wavered. She rested the business end of it on the gunwale of the blue skiff, looking me over. "What if I am? And what were you doing, peeping in my windows?"

"I was looking for a hidden treasure," I said. "His name is Graham Chilly."

Davis maneuvered the skiff up to the side of the *Green Flash* and climbed aboard, holding on to the painter. The pelican ruffled its wings and cocked its head as it backed away. Impressed, no doubt, with her long and elegantly proportioned limbs.

"I don't know any Grahams," she said, looping the painter over a cleat and standing up. "Now please go away."

"How about Zach Malones," I said. "Know any of those?"

"Who are you," she demanded, "and why are you bothering me?"

I introduced myself and told her, very briefly, why it was important to locate Graham Chilly.

"Oh," she said with an unpleasant smile, "you're a narc."

I explained some more. The look in her eye convinced me I wasn't getting through. The pelican didn't like me; therefore, I was a bad guy and not to be trusted.

"Look," I said. "If you see Graham, or know how to get a hold of him, ask him to call home. It's very important."

"If you come out here again," she said, "you better have a search warrant."

Point made, she unlocked the door to the main cabin and slipped inside. The bird shuffled back to its place on the bow, as unperturbed as a figurehead.

When I got back to Land's End, Mutt still had his eyes open. The difference was, he was awake. The cigar was glowing in the side of his mouth and he was working on a fresh bottle of rum.

"There's work if you want it," was the first thing he said. "There's this guy over the Pier House looking to catch bonefish."

"Tell him to try a restaurant."

"I was only passing the information along. I heard you was mixing it up with the Malones, I thought maybe you'd want a diversion. Like working for a living."

Mutt was pointing with his cigar, which is a bad

sign. He wrinkled up his turtle face and made a smart remark about my black eye, and that was it, I was out of there. I walked to the bungalow the long way, to let off steam, and about the time I got there I realized I wasn't mad at Mutt, I was mad at Paula Davis, or maybe at the damn pelican.

I let the door slam behind me and was just snaking a bottle of beer from the fridge when the phone rang.

I held the cold bottle against the bruise on my cheek and said, "I was just about to give you a buzz, Trude. . . . No, I'm not kidding. What I had in mind, if you'd like to come by for supper. You bring the wine, I'll cook. . . . Yes, now you mention it, I *do* have an ulterior motive. What I was hoping, you could bring your log book? . . . Right, just between you and me."

At the kitchen table I poured the beer into a glass, drank half of it, and began to think less about Paula Davis and her pelican and more about Trudy. Everything else aside, she had information I needed. In order not to be a total schmo about it, I had to find a way to use that information without implicating her—or Graham, for that matter.

I tried Kurt Hansen at his office. For reasons known only to the United States government, the call was routed through Miami. When it finally made it back to Key West, he was gone for the day. I dug through my wallet for his card, found his home number scrawled on the back, and punched it.

"Kurt?"

"You first."

"T. D. Stash."

I could hear him inhaling something, and a tinkle of feminine laughter in the background.

"Hey, guy," he said, exhaling so completely I could

practically feel the wind in my ear. "How's it going? You figure out a way to nail that little ketch?"

I told him the ketch was long gone, that I needed an unofficial audience with him in his professional capacity as head of Operations, Drug Enforcement Agency, Lower Keys. To discuss a hypothetical situation.

"My favorite situation." He laughed. "The hypothetical. Tell me, Stash old buddy, are you contemplating something that will require me to hypothetically bust you?"

I laughed it off. Convincingly, I hope.

The bungalow where I make my home is a little one-story job, built of cinder block laid on a slab. It has cool tile floors, a tin roof that drums like Ginger Baker when it rains, and a screened-in porch off the side where I hang my hammock. The yard behind it is just about big enough to swing a cat in, or would be if a gnarled old ficus tree didn't squat in the center, spreading shade so dense the grass doesn't grow. I prefer it that way, a miniature, vine-encrusted jungle that never needs mowing. In one corner is a spot where the sun hits, though, and a frangipani blooms there, producing a unique perfume.

I put three of the big pink blossoms in a glass bowl and set the bowl on the porch table. Then I checked the freezer, found amberjack and crawfish tails, and decided on the tails. The restaurants like to call them Florida lobsters, but they are crawdaddies, plain and simple and just a little tough—more than a little if you make the mistake of overcooking. I defrosted half a dozen, split the shells on the inside curve, and covered them with a marinade, the formula for which I have pledged on my honor not to divulge. Play around with fresh lime juice, extra-virgin olive oil, white vine vinegar, and a finely diced shallot or two, and you just might come up with a crude approximation.

While the tails were soaking I assembled an avocado salad, prepared a batch of yellow rice, and heated up a similar quantity of Cuban black beans. The beans were a cheat, but I haven't yet figured out what Old Man Sánchez, who runs the *bodega* on the corner, does to make his taste the way they do, so we have a deal: I give him money and he gives me the beans in a cardboard container.

I was putting out the plates when a taxi van pulled into the drive. Trudy, carrying gifts.

"Vino," she said, setting a jug on the table. From the string waist of her loose cotton pants she produced a wirebound notebook, flicked the cover with a fingernail, then slipped it into my belt. "Angie is sick, I have to go in at ten for the last part of her shift. So I will be eating and running and whatever else we can fit into three hours."

"We can play Scrabble," I said.

"I'm pissed at Angie. How dare she get intestinal flu on my night off?"

"The nerve," I said. "You pop the wine, I'll get the crawdaddies fired up."

I slipped the tails under the broiler, set the timer, and carried in the salad. Trudy was cupping a frangipani blossom in her hands, drinking in the scent. By a happy accident the pink in the flower matched the pink pattern in her blouse. I began to think that three hours wasn't near long enough.

At first there was a little of that day-after uneasiness that can produce an unnecessary shyness between new lovers. A hesitancy about touching, about acknowledging the physical intimacy. Sex is a pretty tenuous connection, and the mere fact that it has occurred is rarely reason enough to keep two people joined in any meaningful way. Fortunately we'd been casual friends before the lovemaking happened and there was no reason to think the friendship wouldn't deepen, given time. After favoring me with a smile that said we both knew what was happening, and why, Trudy made complimentary noises about the salad and the crawdaddy tails and the wisdom of buying black beans from old man Sánchez.

"So, Trude," I said, topping off her glass of wine, "how do you get from Nebraska to Key West?"

"You want the whole story?"

"That's what I want."

"Well, first you meet a boy in high school, a basketball player with yellow hair and big blue eyes, and then when he joins the navy you follow him to San Diego. After a few months you realize blue eyes and yellow hair go only so far."

I mentioned that she had blue eyes and yellow hair, come to think of it.

"Yes, well. We looked cute, going around together in high school. Everybody said so. It was assumed we would get married and have lots of kids with yellow hair and blue eyes and that the boy kids would play basketball and the girl kids would fall in love with basketball players, other ones, not their brothers, of course."

"Of course."

"And so when we got unmarried I decided I really wasn't ready to go back to Nebraska and explain it to everyone. What I did, I moved off base and got a job as a cocktail waitress. Tom, that's his name, Tom, found someone else who looks a lot like me and right away got her pregnant. When he takes her back to Nebraska for the holidays, I'll bet no one knows the difference."

"At the risk of being impertinent I would venture to say that, yes, they do, too, know the difference."

"Maybe. Anyhow, I met this guy while I was

doing the cocktail thing and he seemed like a really nice guy and before you know it we were living together. More like he was living with me. In my place, I mean. He had this business, he had to shuttle between Fort Lauderdale and San Diego. Something to do with yachts. That's what he always said when I asked, something to do with yachts."

"He was a broker?"

Trudy laughed. "Yeah, you could say that. What happened is I moved into his place in Lauderdale, this canal-front condo he was leasing, and before long I figured out what the something was he did with yachts. He had this connection living aboard a Gulfstar Fifty, and Alvin—that was his name, Alvin, like the chipmunk—old Alvin would take a locked briefcase from the guy on the Gulfstar and he would fly it to San Diego and deliver to another guy who lived aboard a Bertram Sixty in the bay. The yachts get bigger as you go east to west, I guess."

"Alvin wasn't a chipmunk," I said. "He was a mule."

"The point is, Alvin was. Past tense."

"You want to tell me about it?"

"Nothing much to tell," Trudy said, looking into her glass of wine. "One day somebody followed him into a men's room at Miami International and cut his throat and took the briefcase. End of Alvin who had something to do with yachts."

"And something to do with Trudy from Nebraska."

"True," she said, letting the tear drip off the end of her nose. "So what I did, I got in Alvin's BMW and drove south until the road ended. That was three years ago."

She helped me clear the table and stack the dishes in the washer. We had coffee and cognac on the porch and listened to a side of the new Sade album I was touting. You could hear the warm wind blowing through the music, and the flutter of birds returning to roost in the ficus tree as darkness filled the air.

"Your turn," she said after a while. "Who is T. D. Stash?"

"He's a local boy," I said. "He hasn't decided if he wants to make good."

"Has he ever been married?"

"Not in the legal sense," I said, and left it at that.

"I heard this rumor that he once did a little smuggling."

"You're close. He tried, just the one time."

It happened back in the boom-town days of running pot. Before the DEA set up a network, before the AWACs tracked every ship and plane, before the Colombians made a war out of it. I was just another local boy, chasing stone crabs from the Calda Banks to Waltz Key in a leaky stern trapper. Pulling in just enough to make the payments and not a penny more.

"I was working out of this little marina over to Stock Island, only place I could get a slip. Moored next to me is this kid from the 'Glades, couldn't have been more than eighteen, and he's driving this brand new Y & G Fifty-two with big Caterpillar diesels. He's got ten thousand traps sitting on the hill and a couple thousand more in the water and I assume it's his father's boat, right? Eighteen-year-old trap fishermen don't as a rule have four hundred thousand to invest in equipment. Then I hear this kid has bought into one of the fish houses, he's got an interest in wholesale. I'm spending most of my time in the bilge of my little boat trying to keep the engine from shaking loose of the bed, so maybe I wasn't thinking clearly or I would have realized right off you don't get that kind of money skinning 'gators in the big swamp. Every now and then I poke my head up over the gunwale and it seems like that

Y & G Fifty-two is always parked there—the kid is hardly ever fishing those traps. A little light bulb goes on over my head, that the kid is up to something, but mostly I'm too busy working my ass off to give it much thought.

"Then one evening the kid comes aboard my boat and he asks me if I'd like to make a little extra money hauling in a couple of his traps lines. Seems he's too busy with the new wholesale business to do it himself. I say I'm pretty well occupied trying to keep my own lines tended, and he names a price. A very generous price. So I hire a couple of apes to work the stern while I drive and we pull in the kid's trap lines and he pays me. Not only that, he gives me a bonus.

"By now I've heard a lot of stories about exactly what kind of wholesaling he's into, but I figure there's nothing wrong with pulling a man's traps for him. So I get in the last line and stack 'em all on the hill, nice and neat, and the kid shows up with a bottle of tequila and we drink the tequila and he asks me how would I like to make twenty thousand dollars for a night's work, just driving that big boat of his, no heavy lifting?"

Trudy laughing. "I like that," she said. "No heavy lifting."

They say every man has his price. At that particular time mine was twenty thousand dollars. Truth to tell, I'd been waiting for him to ask. Running bales of pot was the thing to do that year. It seemed like half the fishermen in the keys were driving new pickups and ordering big new boats and investing in real estate. I wanted in on the deal. As for moral reservations, I had none: this was marijuana, a mere weed, and the smugglers were men I knew, ordinary fishermen, not organized criminals.

As to risk, there didn't seem to be any.

"Such are the delusions," I said to Trudy, who was facing me in the dark. "You don't get twenty grand to steer a boat without risk. As I found out. Seems the kid from the Everglades was being set up for a fall, and he suspected as much, which was why he hired me to run his boat. What happened is we off-loaded three hundred and fifty bales from a freighter offshore. That's twenty-eight thousand pounds of very pungent Colombian marijuana, more or less sealed in burlap. The damn bales are stacked six high on the rails, eight high in the center, and the boat is wallowing something awful. I'm steering the edge of the Southwest Channel, trying to keep clear of the Coast Guard patrols. In a situation like that you feel like a bug crawling across a glass table. Waiting for the hand to strike, you know?"

Telling the tale again, with only a few embellishments, I could feel that funny cold sweat tickling the small of my back, the metallic taste in my mouth. That old familiar fear.

"We cleared the channel fine and got her inside and I figure, well, the worst is over. I find the little flyspeck key where we're supposed to off-load. The idea is, I was supposed to run the boat up on the beach, the boys waiting there would carry the bales ashore, and the boat would be light enough to back off."

"Sounds primitive," Trudy said.

"Very. It got worse. A lot worse. I run the boat up on the beach, and as soon as I cut the engines, all hell breaks loose. Lights come on all over the island. Two patrol boats suddenly appear. People are screaming through bullhorns. Guys are dumping bales in the water, but it's only knee-deep and you can't flush twenty-eight thousand pounds of pot down the toilet."

"So you're busted."

"What happened, I completely lost my head and just dove in the water and started swimming. Couple of the other guys tried the same thing and got scooped, but somehow they missed me. It was dark out there, scary dark. I dog-paddled until I was about ready to give it up and drown, discovered I was in shallow water, and walked most of the way to Sugarloaf. Up to my waist. Bumped into this big fat nurse shark, who was almost as freaked about it as I was."

"*Jaws*," Trudy said, humming the theme music.

"Anyhow, it takes one hell of a long time to walk eight miles in waist-deep water and I did a lot of thinking."

"You saw the error of your ways," Trudy said, moving closer and smelling of frangipani.

"I did indeed. I thought about how small twenty thousand dollars is compared to, say, a sleeping nurse shark, or three years in Raiford."

"So you gave up the life of crime."

"Well," I said. "More or less."

The guard at the gate to the Truman Annex wanted to know about the windshield. I told him I'd had it removed to improve the air circulation. He looked at the rusty coupe, shrugged, and waved me through. Kurt Hansen runs his operation out of a three-room suite in a new government building adjacent to the Annex. All three rooms are chockablock with computer terminals. Kurt was in the third room, playing imaginary bongos on a desktop. His eyes were red.

"What have you been smoking?" I asked.

"Allergies," he said, smiling enigmatically. "That's what makes my eyes go pink."

"If you say so."

I didn't much like Hansen. He was a wise guy, a slick operator, and a narc. He didn't much like me for the same first two reasons, and because I wouldn't act as an informer. It sort of balanced out and we managed to tolerate each other, so long as our roles were rigidly defined. What we did was trade information. In many respects the act of trading was like a stud poker game, with both of us bluffing on the hole cards.

"I heard you were mixing it up with Zach Malone," he said, grinning and licking his lips. "I thought you were smarter than that, Stash."

I said I hadn't been mixing it up with Zach, that there had been a failure in communications.

"I can see that." His hands went pit-a-pat on the desk. "If what you're going to tell me is you want Zach Malone dusted, we're wasting our time. I would love to nail that beady-eyed son of a bitch, but we can't make a case."

"Never mind Malone," I said. "I'm trying to locate a missing kid."

Without naming names I explained, briefly, about Graham Chilly.

Hansen nodded sleepily. "A Good Samaritan gig, huh? Stash to the rescue, keep the brat from ruining his life?"

"Something like that."

"So what do you want from me?"

I took a piece of folded paper from my pocket and explained that I had six local street addresses. They were the ones Trudy and Graham had called at with the little gift boxes. What I wanted Hansen to do was boot up his file of local drug wholesalers, turn the terminal over to me, and let me see if any of the addresses matched.

"And what do I get?"

"You get my word that I won't call up your superiors in Miami and tell them you've been smoking up the contraband."

Hansen gave me a funny, lazy kind of look. "You wouldn't do that."

"You're right," I said. "I wouldn't. I don't care if you're smoking grandpa's winter socks. All I want to do is get a line on this kid."

Hansen knew his machinery; the ease with which he manipulated the DEA programs was one of the reasons he was top narc in the Lower Keys. He dredged up the appropriate file and showed me how to enter into the cross index. Then he backed off while I did my two-finger trip on the keyboard.

"How complete is this file?" I said after drawing nothing but blanks.

Hansen shrugged. "There's always a few new players turning up, but they don't do business for long before I hear about it. I'd say that file is pretty much up to the minute. Anyone on the island involved in a major shipment in the last six months should be there. The little asterisk after the name," he added gleefully, "means they're under indictment."

"Any other file I should try?"

"You stop playing it so cozy, maybe I can help. Just let me look at the list."

"Like Bartleby said, I prefer not."

"Who the hell is Bartleby?"

"Nobody you know, apparently."

We entered Level Two of the negotiation process, wherein Hansen demanded I tell him everything I knew or he would find a way to haul me before a grand jury, and I countered with an unveiled threat to have his Reeboks torn from his ankles with his feet inside them. Hansen then threw his oldest chestnut on the fire by offering me a job. Steady work, an air-conditioned sedan, full benefits.

"You want," he said, oozing sincerity. "I'll get you a cellular phone."

"Gosh," I said.

"Stash, old buddy, one of these days you're going to have to choose sides."

"You make it sound like *High Noon.*"

"That's a fair analogy. Ever since Operation Everglades it's been Good Guys versus Bad Guys down here. White hats and black hats. You're the only cowboy in the keys who wears a *gray* hat."

"Thanks for the offer, pardner," I said in my best Gary Cooper drawl. "I'd just as soon keep on ridin' the range. Now, if you ainta gonna help me, I best be saddlin' up."

Hansen sighed heavily and clumped his feet up on his desk. "I give up," he said. "My only suggestion, you want to see if any of the people on your list are prime movers, am I correct? Guys who are into the major transactions? Well, maybe you're aiming too high. Maybe this kid you're chasing doesn't have those kind of connections."

With the slightly condescending air of a veteran ball player showing a bush leaguer how to lay down a bunt, Hansen gave me the access code for the local enforcement files. Names and addresses of Key West citizens suspected of retailing narcotics. Neighborhood coke dealers. The nameless extras in Hansen's cowboy world.

"Bingo," I said, staring at the blinking cursor on the screen. "Four out of six."

"See? You're getting worked up over nothing. This juvenile you're so worried about, he's strictly small fry."

Hansen walked me out of his suite, locking locks and talking ragtime. About how the train was leaving without me, how my options were dwindling, how it was time I settled my differences with the establishment and made a career move, like the rest of the grown-ups.

"Fishing for tarpon is no way to make a living,"

he said, shaking his head sadly as he looked at my old wreck of a car. "And this freelance tough-guy stuff, it gets old fast. Get serious, T. D. You keep driving around without a windshield, you'll get bugs in your teeth, know what I'm saying?"

Hansen slipped into his air-conditioned Porsche with the cellular phone. He had the stereo on so loud he didn't hear me dragging the point of a key over his rear quarter-panel. The trouble with guys like Hansen is that they never understand there are worse things than getting bugs in your teeth.

For instance it's a bitch getting paint jobs on a Porsche.

8

LAST call had been given at Zach's Bar. The waitresses, leggy coeds from the community college, were clearing tables. They did not appear, from their attractive physiognomy, to be part of the Malone clan. Unlike the bartender with the kinky red hair, or the bouncer, who had forearms like Popeye and an overbite like Olive Oyl's.

"Seen Bluto around lately?" I asked as he strutted by.

"Huh?"

"Big guy, black beard, mutters a lot."

"We're closing up, mister."

"I don't have to go home, but I can't stay here?"

"You got it."

I got up from the bar stool and made a show of bumping against a table. I lifted the plastic cup of draft beer, burping loudly.

"Sayañara, bee-oot-iful señoritas!" I sang, splashing the beer. The waitresses gave me a wide berth. Popeye veered back. I dropped the beer cup, put one hand on my stomach and the other to my mouth. "Erp! Outa my way!" I lunged for the exit. Popeye back-pedaled, giving me plenty of running room.

Adjacent to the exit was a door marked NO ADMITTANCE. As I had ascertained earlier, it was unlocked. As I staggered around the corner I made a loud gagging noise to discourage anyone from following closely, slipped open NO ADMITTANCE, and pulled the door softly shut.

I stood on the carpeted tread of a steep, narrow stairway. From the attic over the bar came the murmur of voices. Ascending, I began to discern a rhythm in the conversation, a kind of call and response. Someone giving orders. Someone else answering, yes, sir, yes. Yes, sir, yes. I flexed my hands, keeping them loose and ready, and paused at the top of the stairs.

In the attic a couple of rooms had been partitioned off with unpainted wallboard. Light spilled upward from one of the cubicles, illuminating the roof rafters, which converged in a crisscross of shadows. An overhead fan wobbled, blades cutting ineffectually at the heat.

"You tell Jason to keep in line, hear?"

"Yes, sir."

"I don't want to hear no more excuses from that lazy son of a bitch."

"Yes, sir."

"You got any idea how much we got invested in this consignment? Huh? Answer me, boy."

"Not exactly, sir."

The door was made of thin luan plywood, and I could hear them as clearly as if I was in the room. I could also hear someone tromping heavily up the stairs. Time to make a move. I twisted the doorknob, pushed hard, and went into the room faster than I'd intended.

Zach Malone was sitting behind a gray metal desk. The desktop was covered with banded stacks of bills. The redhaired kid from the gill netter stood there with his hands in his pockets. When he saw me his little green eyes hardened, just like his old man's.

"Pardon me, gents," I said. "Is this the pissoir?"

By then Popeye was coming up fast behind me. I flipped the door back and caught him pretty good.

He landed on his backside, more from the surprise than the weight of the door. When I looked at Zach Malone again, he was standing up, all nine feet of him, and holding a pistol.

"Whyn't you have a seat, bubba?" he said. "Right there on the floor."

In truth he wasn't more than six foot six, but the bull neck and the hod carrier's shoulders and the pistol, especially the pistol, made him appear larger than life.

"Hey," I said. "Isn't that a .44 Magnum, like Dirty Harry?"

"On the floor."

"Sure thing." I said. "I been wanting to sit down all night."

"Put your hands behind your head."

So I put my hands behind my head. Popeye got to his feet and started toward me. Zach told him to stop and he did. Zach came out from behind the desk. A .44 Magnum is a big weapon; in his hand it looked small. Then again, when he lined the barrel up with my left eye, it began to take on size.

"You the one keeps that little flat boat over Mutt Durgin's dock. A fish guide."

"That's me."

"What the fuck you doin' busting into my place of business? And how the hell he get by you, Kenny?"

"Don't know, Pa," said Popeye. He edged closer. "Can I kick 'im now?"

"Only the once."

A boot slammed into the small of my back, just missing my kidneys.

"Now, then," Zach said, brushing my nose with the .44, "whyn't you speak up?"

I nodded my willingness to do just that, as soon as I got my breath back.

"Pa, he's the dude come on the boat last night."

"Didn't I just say he was, Roy? Now, you two boys back off and let me handle this. Okay, son, what have you got to say for yourself?"

"I'm looking for a kid. Graham Chilly. I thought you might know where I could find him."

Malone made room on his desk by pushing the stacks of money aside. He settled one haunch down, keeping his eyes and the pistol focused on me.

"Never heard of him," he said.

"I've got a snapshot in my back pocket."

"Take it from him, Kenny."

Popeye squeezed my wrist, just to show me how tough he was.

"He tried to get aboard one of your boats about a week back. At Mallory Wharf," I explained. "Got thrown in the water for his trouble."

Malone studied the picture. Then he laid the .44 on a pile of money and nodded. "Sure. I remember the little shit. What do you want with him?"

"I want to keep him out of trouble. His father is a friend of mine."

"That a fact? And who might his daddy be?"

I explained about Floyd Chilly, his connection to television record promotions and the Palmetto Key Time-Share Resort. I got the impression Malone already knew, that he was extracting some sort of pleasure by making me repeat it.

"Okay," he said when I was done. "Now tell me why y'all think I know where he's at."

"Graham wants to get into the business."

"What business is that?"

"The business you're in."

Malone grinned. There they were, the row of Chiclet-sized teeth I remembered hovering over me after I'd been smacked senseless with the shovel. "Which business? Fishing? The icehouse? The bar?"

"The import business. The big business that finances all your little businesses."

Malone showed me a couple more rows of teeth. I could tell he found me amusing.

"You remember, Zach," I said. "The business you went to prison for, the time you got caught with eight tons of Colombian in a two-stall garage."

The smile froze.

Popeye said, "Can I kick him again, pa?"

"The man is just tryin' to be funny. Ain't that right?"

"I could be funnier if you let me up off the floor."

Malone indicated a metal chair. I got up and went toward it.

"Hold it right there," he said, aiming the .44 again. "First thing I want you to do is peel off that shirt."

"I hate to get undressed in front of strangers," I said.

"Hell," Malone said, "we ain't strangers. Why I want the shirt off is to see if you carryin' a wire."

"I'm not."

"Glad to hear it. Now peel off the shirt. Okay, now turn around slow. Good, put the shirt back on. You understand, I'm a cautious man, T.D. Is that what they call you, T.D.? What's them initials stand for, anyhow?"

"Terribly Dashing."

He was grinning again, and that was an improvement. "You a real comedian, Mr. Terrible. Now go on, set yourself down in that chair and tell me again why I should go out of my way to help you locate this boy."

While two of his brood of sons looked at me with eyes the color of eel grass, I gave Zach Malone an edited version of my Graham Chilly theory: the means-well only child who tried to buy friendship with gifts of cocaine and who now meant to rescue his family from financial straits by setting up a major drug transaction.

"How much of this do you know," Malone asked, "and how much of it is pure guesstimation?"

"I know he's been in contact with certain retailers. Coke pushers, mostly. And that he approached you."

Malone rested the .44 on the desk again. He shuffled the stacks of money absentmindedly. Popeye was bored, his eyelids flickered sleepily, but Roy, the one who'd smacked me with the shovel, followed the exchange with interest. His expression, regarding me, was strangely blank. As if I was a bug and he an exterminator considering the best way to make me go away.

"Well," Malone said at last, "won't do no harm to tell you what happened."

"*Pa*," Roy warned.

"Hold yer water, boy. I'm just gonna tell Mr. Terrible here how certain folks on this island like to think the worst of a man. Like to think Zach Malone is still involved in the business that once got him throwed in jail. Well, there ain't no truth in it. Not a bit, which is the main reason I lost my temper and had the little fool Graham run off the gangplank. The other reason is because the boy had it all twisted around. If he knowed anything at all, it was that back when I *was* briefly involved in that business—which, you understand, I ain't involved no more—all I ever done was run bales of pot. Never had nothing to do with no cocaine. That stuff is for them wild-ass greaseballs up in Miami. For white gentlemen down here in the keys, it is strictly marijuana by the ton."

It was a nice little homily and I think he even believed some of it. Zachary Malone gone straight, his reputation tainted by cruel rumors. What made it hard to swallow were the stacks of cash on his desk and the ease with which he held a man at gunpoint.

"So Graham is trying to put a coke deal together?"

"The boy wants to make a whole lot of money fast. You can't do that with the marijuana business. With marijuana you need a lot of help, you intend to move it by the ton. A whole network of helpful people. And the money don't come on the instant. It takes time, understand me? The goods have to reach the market, then people what helped get their little reward."

"Pa," Roy said, "you don't have to tell this dude nothin'."

"I knows I don't, boy. But I am choosing to give him a message, and the message is that any person coming uninvited into Malone territory and suggesting that Zachary C. Malone is in the business of transporting cocaine is going to get throwed through the air right sudden. Suggestions like that are dangerous to everyone, Mr. Terrible. You understand what I'm telling you?"

I did indeed. Malone was a big-time marijuana teamster, his transportation business well-established and -defended, and he didn't want anyone—not the DEA and most particularly not certain dangerous elements in Miami—to get the idea he was moving into another line of endeavor. To do so would be to risk violent interference with certain foreign elements in the Miami area.

"That's why my boys treated you so rough last night," he said. "It weren't meant personal. They would have done the same to any stranger tryin' to come aboard."

At the mention of rough treatment Popeye came back to life and muttered something to his brother. They both grinned at me. It was the kind of grin you get across the campfire from a pair of wolf cubs.

"Okay," I said. "Before you gave Graham the heave-ho, did he give any indication of where he might go next? Who he intended to contact?"

"There ain't nobody going to deal with him," Malone said. "But the boy couldn't get it through his head. He was talking crazy about this 'independent contractor' he knew. A Marielito scum they call Zarpa."

"Is that a real name?"

Malone shrugged. "I don't pay no attention. All I know, this Zarpa is one bad actor. A psycho likes to hurt people. Spent most of his life in a Cuban jail, and for good reason. The boy gets himself mixed up with that jackal, you can kiss his skinny ass goodbye."

Malone locked the Dirty Harry cannon in a desk drawer and stood up. End of interview. It was obvious his spawn were disappointed when dear old dad elected to escort me out himself. Going down the steep stairway, he loomed over me, his hand gripping my shoulder without any particular force. In the parking lot he was cordial, as if I had been forgiven my trespass.

"Good luck with the boy," he said, glancing up to where the light shone out of an attic window over his saloon. "My impression, he don't mean no particular harm. Got his head inflated with the white powder, is all. But one thing I did hear, Mr. Terrible Dashing, the boy ain't the only one in the family with an unhealthy interest in cocaine."

"Yeah? Where'd you hear that?"

In the darkness I couldn't make out his face. Instinct told me he was wearing that swampy Malone smile as he said, "Why, a little birdie told me, son. A cute little birdie."

9

I sat on my porch in the dark, knowing I would have to sort some of it out before sleep could come. Sipping at a beer without any real interest, I was aware of the fading scent of the frangipani blossoms on the table. Which in turn reminded me of Trudy, who was ferrying late-night revelers around the island in her taxi van.

The taxi, Graham delivering little gift boxes of cocaine, all done up in wrapping paper and blue ribbons. What bothered me was the absurdity of his carrying coals to Newcastle, as it were. What had the kid been trying to do, giving gifts of cocaine to half a dozen coke pushers? Was he bribing them? Paying them back? Looking to make a big score? That would be the obvious conclusion, except that, according to Kurt Hansen's computer files, all of the addresses from Trudy's log of that night belonged to small-time dealers. Low-level pushers who did not have access to "prime movers," as Hansen liked to call them, which meant it was unlikely any of the gift recipients could help Graham put together a major transaction.

It just didn't make sense. I didn't have Zach Malone's sources. Little birdies did not talk to me. Trying to figure out what was going on in the world of narcotic wholesalers/retailers was like looking into a tidal pool: I could see big fish and little fish, but my perception was skewed by the ceaselessly changing surface of the water.

The beer was warm by the time it occurred to me that maybe I was too late. Maybe Graham had already made his deal for quantity and was now trying to dispose of it. Maybe he wasn't looking to buy, but to sell. If his prime mover was an outside source, Graham would need buyers who were not already committed to an established network of distribution. If that was the case, the ten-gram packages he had delivered by taxi might be samples, not gifts or bribes.

"Take a sniff of this, boys, there's a lot more where it came from. . . ." Oh, yes, it made sense if you looked at the fish from that angle. But was it the truth? Where did Malone fit into it, and why was he warning me about someone else in Graham's little family? And who among them wielded a machete? And why had he made a special point to mention a Marielito bandit known as Zarpa?

It went round in my head until the dizziness carried me down. I fell asleep there on the porch and slept in a confusion of jagged dreams, until morning woke me with a sky as blue as a twelve-bar riff of B. B. King.

The callow youth who ran the back-order desk at the automotive supply on Stock Island didn't, in his words, know dick about my windshield.

"An old junker like that, it's hard to find parts," he added, staring at the computer screen as he fingered a ZZ Top earring. "We put in a request on the open file, like we told you, but none of the wholesalers have responded."

"This is a '67 Coupe de Ville. A classic car."

He nodded. "If you say so."

"I do," I said, "say so. Isn't there a custom supply source you can try? A clearinghouse?"

"More money," he said. "Those outfits charge what they call a finder's fee."

"Fine. I'm willing to pay what they call a finder's fee if it means I get a new windshield. Or an old windshield, even."

Didn't-know Dick began clacking away on his terminal, looking too bored to live, to hip to die.

"You care if it's tinted?"

"Any color but pink."

Dick glared. His hair was tinted pink at the ends. To get revenge he lit up a clove cigarette while he waited for the screen to answer. It smelled like an electrical fire that had been doused with whorehouse perfume.

I stepped outside, stored up oxygen, and returned.

"We got a match. A chop yard in Alabama. They'll ship, but I got to tell you the dunnage charge is ferocious."

"How long will it take to get here?"

"Depends."

"On what?" I said.

"On how long it takes."

That was the way the day started. It was enough to make you want to kick a puppy dog. It suited my mood to have George Thorogood & The Destroyers blasting "Bad to the Bone" on the tape deck. On the Gulf side there was not even a breath of wind; the sea was bottle-green and smooth. The heat of noon pressed down, arid and mean. A small voice in my stomach whined that I had neglected to breakfast. If my instincts about Graham Chilly were right, there wasn't time for such amenities. The sand was running through the glass, as fine and sudden as uncut cocaine.

I hung a right off the Overseas Highway, heading for the commercial fishing wharves on Stock Island. Cuban side. It had been a while and I made a few wrong turns before locating the correct access road.

When the smell of crescote got hot and thick, I knew I was close.

On a narrow strip of land between canals, the Valdez family was hard at work, dipping traps. The old man was standing under the work shed roof, directing traffic. A trap was passed from one Valdez hand to the next until it arrived at the worktable, where one of the Valdez girls scraped off the barnacles with an iron bar. As the trap moved down the line, one of her brothers pulled off loose slats. Another brother fastened on new slats, using an air nailer. Then the old man gave it a final inspection before one of his huskier boys, wearing elbow-length black rubber gloves, heaved the rebuilt trap into a drum of warm creosote. After soaking, each trap was removed, drained, and passed hand to hand to the stacks of traps that made a maze of the wharf area.

I parked the coupe where it wasn't likely to be picked up and dipped. The old man saw me and waved, an ivory smile flashing from a sun-burned face.

"*El Tiburón*," he shouted. "*El Tiburón regresó.*"

This was followed by a torrent of words, mostly directed toward his wife, who was toiling in the camp kitchen.

The shark returns, that much I understood. While I usually get by pretty well with my schoolboy Spanish, old man Valdez' dialect is a puzzle. We communciate through one or more of his eight sons, all of whom speak perfect English, when they are so inclined. Son number one is Rey, who peeled off the long rubber gloves and took my hand.

"How's it go, man?" he asked. "You just in time, we about to sit down to dinner."

Ray is my height and carries a lot more weight, mostly around the middle, which makes him about twice as massive as the old man, who is skin and bones and tougher than a conch shell. It was Rey who'd gotten stranded during the Mariel boatlift, when he'd gone over to take some of his cousins off the big island. At the time I happened to be in a position to get him out of a serious jam, and the old man has never forgotten the favor. I was El Tiburón because I'd eaten my share and more of a mako at the impromptu celebration following Rey's return, and because the old man couldn't figure out how to pronounce my given name.

Rey's wife, Tina, took off her apron, brushed the hair from her eyes, and kissed me on the mouth. Believe me, it's a big deal when a Cuban wife kisses another man on the mouth, especially if that man is an Anglo. Under the wrong circumstances it can lead to the kiss of a knife.

"No mako today, Stash," Rey said, aiming a slap at his wife's impressive backside. "Only chicken."

Only chicken was platter after platter of deep fried, breaded in cornmeal and garlic, served with white rice, vinaigrette salad, and cold beer. It was one hell of a breakfast. I finally had to push my plate away before I fell into it face first for an unscheduled siesta. The old man kept beaming at me as I ate—he never seemed to eat much of anything, but he expected everyone else in the family to feed until bloated. When I finally convinced him I couldn't chew another morsel, he brought out the espresso and handed me a toothpick.

While the rest of the family went back to the trap work, Rey and his father sat with me under the shed roof, drinking coffee. The old man said something and pointed to my bruised eye.

"He says, who did that to you?"

"Tell him I was looking through a keyhole."

"He says maybe you need some help, finding this keyhole that punched you."

"Rey," I said, judging the time had come to get down to business, "do you know a Marielito con named Zarpa?"

Rey looked surprised, then angry. "What do you know of Zarpa?"

"Zarpa?" the old man chirped. "¿Quién es este Zarpa?"

"Easy, Papa." Rey leaned forward toward me and said, "Do you know this man? Have you seen him?"

"No," I said. "All I know is he's supposed to be dangerous."

I showed Rey the snapshot of Graham Chilly and ran down the facts as I knew them. He studied the picture, sighed, and handed it back.

"Come with me," he said. "I, too, have a photograph."

In the work shed was a tiny alcove fitted out as an office. Trap-fishing is a business like any other, and Rey had to keep ledgers, books, receipts, the usual paper effluvia. Thumbtacked to the raw Sheetrock wall were various licenses and tax stamps and a lot of family snapshots. Rey drew my attention to a glossy eight-by-ten.

"This was taken last September, at the feast of La Santa de la Caridad," he said with a sigh. "Naturally, everyone from the community was in attendance. The food, Madre de Dios, it is enough to split your belly. More than enough for whatever person chooses to attend. One of these people, he is the one who calls himself Zarpa. This one here."

It was a crowd shot, a hundred or more people around a gaily decorated banquet table. Some of the old-timers were decked out in the fringed mantillas of days gone by. If the dazed smiles were any indication, a good time had been had by all. The man Rey pointed out was standing to one side, wearing jeans cut-off at the knee and a ragged white T-shirt. In the photograph his face was somewhat indistinct, partly in shadow. All you could really make out were the dark, glittering eyes, the shock of shoulder-length black hair, and high cheekbones. A rawboned, wiry man who had the look of someone who could move quick. The eyes, as opaque as chunks of coal, gave away nothing.

"If this boy Graham is doing a deal with Zarpa," Rey said, "he is in very big trouble."

"So he's a bad hombre?"

Rey nodded. "He likes to kill people. They call him Zarpa because he keeps his fingernails real long, like claws. For a long time after the boat lift he was in the detention camp, classified as an undesirable because of his prison record, and then somehow he gets a sponsor. Later I hear that someone in the sponsor's family died in a way that was not fully understood. We heard of this later, unfortunately. What happened, last year there was an incident with one of the children. A little girl. She is okay now, but it is forbidden for Zarpa to come around here."

"And if he does?"

Rey shrugged. "This thing with the little girl was very serious. If Zarpa comes around the community, he will be made to disappear. He knows this."

"Any idea where he is now?"

Rey shook his head, "Last I heard, he was going north. Miami or Tampa, I don't know. Now perhaps he is back, which is very dangerous for him. The little girl's father, you understand? But this man Zarpa is a crazy thing. If you find him, kill him."

"I surely hope it won't come to that," I said, thinking of the machete that had hacked up my car seat.

Rey gripped my wrist. "I am speaking true to you, my brother. This is a man who must be killed, and very quick, too, or he will kill you first."

"You're scaring the hell out of me, Rey."

"That's good," he said. "Now you don't forget."

10

THERE was a familiar, acrid-sweet scent inside the house. High-grade marijuana, ignited not long before I entered through the back porch. With Rey Valdez' warning in mind, my first thought was of an intruder. I closed the screen door with care and walked lightly over the tiled floor toward the closet where I keep my extra fishing gear. There is a blue plastic tool box on the top shelf. In the bottom of the toolbox is an old but serviceable .38 Smith & Wesson revolver. I filled the chamber, lifted the hammer, and followed my nose.

Trudy was asleep on my bed. The last tendrils of smoke wafted up from the ashtray on the nightstand. I eased the hammer down and slipped the .38 into a bureau drawer before going to the bed. Her eyes opened when I touched her shoulder.

"I came by to say hello," she said sleepily. "What time is it?"

"Midafternoon. You done for the day?"

She shook her head. A strand of corn-yellow hair clung to her lower lip. "Gotta go back in at five, off at midnight. I was wondering, do you want to help me take a nap?"

"Well, I'm pretty busy right now."

"That's okay," she said, starting to sit up. "I should have—"

I eased her back down. "I reckon I can find the time, Nebraska."

Every now and then you need a reminder of what's really important. Besides, it is bad luck to throw a beautiful woman out of your bed. Worse than breaking a mirror, or stepping on a crack, or being third on a match. I'm not the superstitious type, but there are situations that demand making an exception.

As situations went, Trudy was . . .

Come to think of it, none of your business. Suffice to say we napped, eventually, and just before leaving for work she asked me if I'd like to give Smathers Beach another try.

"Moonrise at midnight?" I asked. "Love under the swaying palms? Is that what you have in mind?"

"That's what I have in mind. Sort of starting over."

"You ask all your boyfriends to meet you on the beach?"

"Only one," she said. "So far. And he stood me up the first time."

"I'll be there," I promised, making the Boy Scout pledge sign. "Come hell or high water."

Little did I know.

When I was in fifth grade I had a friend named Nelson. Like me, Nelson was an only child. His father was alive, unlike mine, but Nelson had neither seen nor heard from him. We had that and a profound love for comic books in common. *Superman*, *Green Lantern*, *Tales from the Crypt*. We traded copies, sent away for prizes, imagined we would grow up to be superheroes.

I grew up to be an unlicensed troublemaker. Nelson Kerry grew up to be a cop. Lieutenant Kerry of the Key West Police Department, to be exact. We had long since ceased to be close friends. Partly, I'm convinced, because old Nelly is afraid he'll have to arrest me one of these days.

The lieutenant was in his office on Angela Street. He was sitting at a typewriter when I found him. Not typing, just staring at the machine as if he wanted to melt it with his eyes, like Superman.

"You took your time," he said. "The way it usually happens, someone gets assaulted, they come right in and file the complaint."

"I'm not here to file a complaint, Nel."

"No? Then I suppose you're here to report you did wrongfully take the life of one Zachary C. Malone. Which is why you'd been better off filing the assault complaint first. Maybe then they'd drop the charge to manslaughter, on account of Malone is an immovable object."

"Forget it, Nel. Zach and I are good buddies now."

"Yeah?" Kerry pushed back from the typewriter and fished in his pocket for a cigarette, which meant he wasn't in one of his quitting periods. "Glad to hear it. He's a heck of a guy, Zach is. Sweet, docile, forgiving."

"He's a saint, Nel. A pillar of the community."

"So," Kerry said, inhaling deeply, "you're not here to con me into putting the cuffs on Malone, you must want something else."

"Gosh, I'm really hurt you'd think that. Like I only come by when I need a favor."

Kerry was up to his old trick, making donuts out of Camels. "I'm waiting," he said between huffs.

"You borrowed a *Batman* from me about twenty years ago. I want it back."

Kerry grinned, punching at the rings of smoke with an extended forefinger. "Good old Batman. What a crime-fighter *that* guy was. Sad to say, my mother threw all my comic books out while I was in the army. So I guess that's another thing you can blame on Vietnam."

"I'm devastated," I said. "To make up for losing my *Batman* I think you owe me a favor."

"This is getting to be a familiar routine, T.D. It's getting old."

"So are we all, Nelly. Little by little. What I'd like to know, if you can help, is where I might locate a certain individual."

I told him what I knew of the man called Zarpa, including his banishment from the Cuban community.

Kerry nodded, lighting his next cigarette from the butt in his mouth. "I heard about that. Burning the little girl with matches. They brought her into the hospital. Naturally I went down to see the family. No way to get them to bring charges, of course. Not through an Anglo cop like me. Handle it among themselves. I got the impression the guy was dead meat, he ever went around there again."

"The Cubans take a hard line on child molesters," I said.

"They take a hard line on everything," Kerry said. "On the other hand, I don't think anyone in the department would get too excited if the guy came to an untimely end. Not that I would ever countenance vigilante justice, you understand."

"I understand perfectly."

"So what do you want with this creep Zarpa?"

"I think he may be involved with a major drug transaction."

"No way," Kerry said firmly. "No one down here would deal with an animal like that. Maybe up in Miami."

"Agreed. It might be a rip-off. A kid I'm looking for may be mixed up in it and I want to find him before he gets burned."

"Like the little girl."

I nodded.

"If I knew where this Zarpa character was at, I'd tell you. I haven't the foggiest. So who's the kid?"

By then I had my Graham Chilly story down line for line. I left out the part about delivering little packages of whoopee powder to the local pushers, because Nelly would want the names and I didn't feel like explaining that he already had them in his computer file. He would want to know how I knew that, which would entail mentioning Kurt Hansen of the DEA, and Nelly loathed the DEA because they treated him like what he was: a small-town cop.

"The old man came in here last week. Makes those record albums they sell on the tube? A genuine celebrity. Not a bad guy, really. I told him we'd put an all-points on the boy's car, which we did. It hasn't been recovered. What he really wanted, Famous Floyd, was for us to conduct a manhunt for the kid. I told him that we weren't equipped for manhunts this year and that he should get his lawyer to recommend someone from the private sector. Who I guess is you."

"You were always a good guesser, Nel."

"What makes you think the boy didn't just take off to see the world?"

"Could be he did," I said.

"You still have that Smith and Wesson you bought off me? My advice, if you're determined to run down this bad-news Marielito, you best keep it handy. That's strictly off the record, of course."

"Of course."

"And you know if I pull the kid in first, and he's holding, I'll bust him."

"You're only doing your job."

"That's how it works," he said.

From the cop shop I walked over to Mallory Square

and found Fletcher Brown sleeping under a palm-frond sombrero. His Conch Republic T-shirt was twisted up, exposing a brown, hairless belly and a white appendix scar.

I tapped the brim of the sombrero. Fletch's right hand did a crab walk over the grass, located my sneakers, and withdrew.

" 'Lo, Stash," he said from under the brim.

"Had your supper, Fletch?"

"Never eat supper."

"How about breakfast?"

He came out from under the sombrero, expressing enthusiasm for the idea, the concept, the philosophy, of breakfast. As he walked over to Duval Street, I noticed he was limping.

"I think it may be gout," he explained earnestly. "I ain't been taking my vitamins lately. You know how you get out of the habit?"

We sat at the counter in Shorty's while Fletch devoured eggs, corned-beef hash, sausages, a pint of fresh-squeezed orange juice, and a side of grits. He paused now and then to dab at his wispy gray goatee with a paper napkin. I was still recovering from the Valdez banquet and made do with coffee and a slice of Key-lime pie.

When Fletch had topped off his vitamin level with a second large juice, I asked him about Zarpa. As soon as I mentioned the clawlike fingernails, his eyes shifted away.

"He used to come around the dock," he said. "Ain't seen him in a while."

"How about Graham, would he have known Zarpa?"

Fletch shrugged, absently stroking at his generously proportioned nose. "Might have, I guess. I never put the two of them together. You wouldn't put nobody together with Zarpa. The man is an animal. A creepy-crawly type."

I asked him to explain.

"You see him, you get this creepy-crawly feeling. I don't know if it's those Fu Manchu fingernails, or the look in his eye. But he gives off this very unhealthy aura."

As we walked back to the square, Fletcher's limp had improved. Still there, but not so noticeable. His silver-gray ponytail swung like a pendulum as he greeted the street vendors. The Conch Train was delivering tourists to the dock for the sunset madness. Up ahead, burning tapers were sailing in a fiery arc from a juggler's hands. Two costumed men were chasing each other on tall unicycles. Someone in a Ronald Reagan mask was doing backflips and braying like an ass, which made for a credible impersonation.

"If I wanted to find Zarpa, where would I look?"

"You could try under a rock. Or maybe in a swamp. I'm telling you, Stash, the man gives off weird vibrations."

"Probably result of a vitamin deficiency."

"Laugh if you want, man. The dude has some kind of sickness in him. Inside he's all twisted up. He come on to me once, about how would I like to make a few dollars helping him do this certain thing? I say, what certain thing, and he get's this look, man, like to make my blood run cold. I give him a couple of numbers and he let me alone, but I could tell he wanted to score a lot more than two lousy joints."

"A rip-off artist?"

Fletcher shrugged. "I got that impression. Last time Zarpa come around, he was trying to jive this dude who needed to move an oh-zee of toot. This was definitely an uncool dude, right? Living in a van with expired Louisiana plates, talking ragtime about this nose candy he needed to unload. I don't know if he was really holding an ounce, but he and Zarpa drove off somewhere, I ain't seen neither one since."

That seemed to be an odd thing about the man who called himself Zarpa. People went off with him and were not seen since. I left Fletch at Mallory Dock, where he blended into the crowd like a water spot on a madras jacket, and went home. When I got there the phone was ringing.

"You better come right away," Floyd Chilly said in a strained baritone. "They called about an hour ago."

"Who called?"

"The kidnappers," he said. "The ones who got Graham."

11

A translucent blue twilight had settled over Palmetto Key. I had to get out and open the gate myself. There was a light on in the guard shack, and a transistor blasting a conga tune on Radio Martí, but no security guard. I leaned in through the missing windshield of the coupe, took the .38 out of the glove compartment, and tucked it in the waist of my jeans before pushing open the iron gate. The guard not being on station bothered me. That and the incessant burring of the insects.

I put the car in gear and without touching the accelerator pedal let it roll down the long driveway. Gravel crunched under the fat tires. I wasn't sure what I was listening for. Footsteps from the swamp, maybe, or the keen sound a machete makes as it slices air.

The front door at the main house was open. Light spilled down the spiral of steps. An angry, Spanish-speaking voice came from inside, sounding brittle and indignant. When Floyd Chilly came through the door there was no indication that he noticed the weapon in my hand.

"It's bad," he said, his voice a hoarse whisper. "I just know it is. I got this real bad feelin'."

His wife was in the big, overdecorated living room, perched on a stool at the bar. She had a glass in her hand and she was pointing it at the security guard, who answered with another torrent of Spanish. I tucked the .38 back in my waist, covered it with the tail of shirt, and let Floyd precede me into the living room. As we approached the bar the security guard took off his cap, threw it on the white rug, and stomped it with the heel of his boot.

"*La tumba de mi sagrada madre*," he shouted, "*que es la verdad.*"

"He swears he is telling the truth," I said to Reggie.

"I understand that much, thank you," she said, putting the glass down on the bar top. "Now, Carlos, please calm yourself. I am not accusing you of lying to me. I simply want to know why this man on the telephone knew all about you."

Carlos picked up his cap and looked at it sorrowfully. He was young, not much older than Graham, perhaps, and so thin he'd had to punch an extra hole in the belt of his agency uniform. Under the mistaken notion that I could keep up with him, he spoke rapidly, slapping the cap against his narrow chest in punctuation.

"Slow down, son," Floyd said. "You was speakin' good English before we got that call."

"Hokay," the guard said, gulping air. "So you want to fire me, hokay. But I say to you, I don't know nothing about this thing."

After a while I was able to sort out the sequence of events. Reggie was out on the patio and Floyd had taken the call. The voice was threatening, heavily accented. Graham's name was repeatedly mentioned, but Floyd was not sure about what, exactly, the voice was demanding that he do. After about five nerveracking minutes he was able to understand that he was being instructed to bring the security guard to the phone. This Reggie did, calling him on the intercom. With the guard as translator, the conversation continued. As conversations go, it was virtually one-sided.

According to the anonymous caller, Graham was being held by a group of desperate men. *Desesperados*, the security guard had kept repeating. A ransom was demanded. One million dollars in cash. Under no circumstances were the police to be informed, or their son would be killed immediately. They were to get the money together and await delivery instructions.

"How many voices?" I asked the guard. "Did you speak with more than one man?"

"No. The one only."

"Did he put Graham on the phone?"

"No."

"What did he say that made you think he was not alone?"

The guard snugged the cap down. It made him look even younger, like a boy wearing his big brother's uniform. "Because he say 'we.' We want money. We have Mr. Graham. We will kill him. Like that, you understand?"

"Did you recognize the voice?"

He shook his head, looking at the floor.

"The man was speaking Spanish. Was he Mexican? Puerto Rican? Cuban? Could you tell?"

"Of course. Like me, he is Cuban. A *campesino*."

"A peasant? How could you tell?"

"I know how a *campesino* speak. Do you think I am a stupid man?"

"No," I said. "Did he know your name, this *campesino*?"

"He knows only that there is a guard who speaks Spanish. As I am telling Mrs. Chilly, it might be that he knows this from Graham."

"Could you hear Graham in the background? Anything?"

"Only the man. He is very loud, shouting into the telephone."

In schoolboy Spanish I thanked him and asked that he return to the guard shack and report immediately if anyone attempted to enter the grounds.

To hear that cool, carefully modulated tone of hers was to assume Regina Chilly was firmly in control. A glance, however, revealed the corded tightness in her throat, the tremble in her wrists and hands, and eyelids that fluttered so rapidly the mascara was starting to smear. She was frightened. The way she kept working her tongue around her mouth, searching for moisture, made me think she might be high on something other than adrenaline. I don't think Floyd noticed her at all. He mainly concentrated on the telephone, a pink lacquered job that squatted on the bar like an obscene, oversized bug.

"I suggest we bring in the FBI," I said. "When they call again, the FBI can set up a trace."

"He said no cops," Reggie said woodenly. She had the glass in both hands, using it as an anchor to steady the shakes.

"The other option is to pay up."

"We'll do it," Floyd said, staring at the pink telephone. "Whatever they want, we'll give it to them."

"Oh, for God's sake," Reggie said, letting her voice go. "A million dollars? We haven't got that kind of money."

"We'll get it. We'll find it. I can, I was just thinking, maybe I can get hold of Louis Vance in Nashville."

Reggie gulped at the drink and stood up. She made a point of not meeting my eyes. "Floyd, dear, Louis Vance is an accountant. That's all he is, a glorified accountant. He doesn't have the authority. Or the money."

"An advance on royalties," Floyd said, talking mostly to himself. "Louis could fix it."

"We're living on the advance, Floyd. Remember?"

I said, "Federal Bureau of Investigation. Shall I make the call or would you rather do it?"

Floyd placed his big, truck-farmer hands protectively over the pink telephone. He shook his head slowly. "They said no cops. We'll do what they want. Exactly what they want."

"Okay," I said. "Fine. Let's think about this whole thing for a couple minutes. Mind if I get myself a drink?"

No one minded. I poured from a bottle of fine Kentucky bourbon. The Chillys were no more than a yard apart, yet they might have been on different planets. Nothing was happening between them—no touching, no worried hugs, no spark of real argument, even. They were weaving their own cocoons, shutting out reality.

After the first sip of bourbon I said, "What happened to the girl, Mrs. Chilly?"

Reggie looked blank. "What girl?" she said.

"The girl Graham ran off with. The reason you weren't worried about him being in trouble."

"Maybe he was lying about the girl. Maybe—"

"It's something to do with drugs," Floyd said, cutting her off. "Jist like I was afraid. Something went wrong and now they holding the boy."

I told Floyd I thought his assessment of the situation was probably accurate. Graham had been all over the waterfront, attempting to organize a major transaction, and there was reason to believe he had crossed paths with a rip-off artist. A crude con man who used muscle rather than wit to make his score.

"The bad news is that this man Zarpa is extremely dangerous and unpredictable. The good news is that he's probably working alone. If I've got it right, he convinced your son he could deliver a quantity of cocaine. Either he was planning to steal the coke or he never intended to make delivery. I don't know what went wrong with the drug deal and right now it doesn't really matter. What matters is that our rip-off artist turned kidnapper wants cash. A whole lot of it."

"We'll get him some," Floyd said, slapping his hand on the bar.

"Maybe I can help with the money," I said. "But first there's something we need to determine. We have to find out if Graham is still alive."

This seemed a reasonable-enough priority. I was caught flat-footed by the slap that scorched the side of my face. I grabbed Reggie's wrist, then let it go. Her eyes were burning cold, snow-blinded with coke. I wondered if she had gotten high before or after the call. Floyd was startled, confused. He reached for his wife and was shaken off.

"This is *not* happening," Reggie said. "My son has *not* been kidnapped. There has been some sort of misunderstanding, that's all. He has certainly *not* been killed, and it is beastly of you to say so."

Mrs. Chilly had plenty of muscle built into that petite frame. She had struck with a force somewhere between an enraged slap and a KO punch. Much harder and I would have had to drink through a straw.

I worked on the bourbon and waited until she had finished flailing around.

"All I meant," I said, "the next time he calls, have him bring Graham to the phone. Insist on it. For all we know, he doesn't have your son at all. Maybe Graham has really run off with a girl and the extortionist is simply using his absence as a leverage of fear."

But Floyd was shaking his head. "There weren't no girl, Stash. At least not one he run off with."

"Floyd," Reggie said in a warning tone.

"Just tell us what to do," he said.

The Radio Shack at the Winn-Dixie Plaza was closing up when I got there. The manager, who later told me he was a retired air-force colonel, had the keys in the door and the deposit bag tucked under his arm. When I tapped him on the shoulder he dropped the bag and jumped.

"It's mostly checks," he said, staring at my waist. "Hardly worth bothering."

I looked down. The grip of the .38 was clearly visible where my shirt had come untucked. The manager was breathing hard, taking in more air than he was letting out. Hyperventilating. I started talking fast, explaining how appearances can be deceiving and how I was but a would-be customer. He kept breathing hard, his eyes going glassy. I was tempted to hand him the gun before he collapsed like a vented dirigible, but I thought he might shoot first and exhale later.

Finally I picked up the deposit bag and made him take a hold of it. Physical possession of the receipts seemed to calm him. Eventually he listened. After seeing the color of my money he agreed to reopen the store and sell me certain items. A portable tape deck, blank cassettes, a telephone mike.

"This is an emergency," I said, handing over the cash. "Life or death."

"Anything you say, mister."

Thirty minutes later I had the gear attached to the Chillys' pink telephone. As anyone with an answering machine knows, there is nothing illegal about recording your own phone calls. Of course, it was not as effective as putting a trace on the incoming calls, but there was no way to do that without bringing in, at the very least, the local constables.

"It's very simple," I explained to Floyd. Reggie,

he had informed me, was having a bath for her "nerves." "Anytime the phone rings, you lock down this button before you answer. It's a long shot, but we may get something in the background that will give us an idea where he's got your stepson. At the very least we'll have his voice on tape and voice-prints are as good as fingerprints, this ever gets to court."

"He's going to want us to get Carlos to talk to him again."

"Fine. Do what he says. Agree to anything, so long as he let's you talk to Graham. Tell him it will take a couple of days to get the cash together."

"Hell," Floyd said, staring uncertainly at the tape deck, "that could take forever. We're in hock right up to our eyeballs, son."

I promised to do what I could.

It was getting on toward midnight when I finally ran Kurt Hansen to ground at the Chart Room. He was playing darts with two of the local politicos. All three were drinking tequila out of shot glasses. There was no foolishness with lemons or salt. Hansen insisted I down one before he would agree to take leave of the dart board or his fat-cat friends.

"I tried you at home," I said, raising my voice to be heard over a Barry Manilow medley that was playing at excruciating volume. "They said you were out."

"They?" Hansen shouted. " 'Mean Rosita?"

"Whoever answered."

"Rosita, my new maid."

"You've got a maid?"

Hansen nodded. The nod was exaggerated. He'd been drinking for a while and it showed. "Doesn't everybody?" he said as I steered him out to the patio. "Rosita's a Nicaraguan. Prob'ly a fucking Sandinista. All I know for sure is the fucking part."

The patio outside the Chart Room was part of the Pier House complex. We followed a boardwalk around an illuminated swimming pool.

Hansen wasn't staggering, not exactly, but he was having trouble keeping his designer sunglasses perched on the crown of his head. "Let's go see the fishies," he suggested, picking up the pace. "The pretty little fishies."

There were underwater spots rigged under the pier itself and from the veranda you can lean on the rail and look down into pools of blue light. When the water is clear, which is most of the time, hundreds of fish circle. Snook, jack, triggerfish, lots of mullet, a small shark or two, all circling without pause. You can fall into a trance, staring down at the fish. Hansen tossed a penny over the side. A snook charged, then changed its mind and glided by, letting the penny spin to the bottom.

"Guess it must be heavy," he said.

"Heavy?"

"Whatever it is made you chase me down this time of night."

"It's nothing much," I said. "I just want to borrow a million dollars."

"See that one?" he said, pointing down. "The one with the funny head? What kind of fish is that?"

"Baby hammerhead," I said.

"You're kidding, a hammerhead shark? It can't be more than a foot long."

"They start out small. I don't think it matters about the denomination. Twenties would be fine. What's important is that it look like a hell of a lot of money."

"What?" Hansen said. "What are you talking about?"

"The million bucks I need to borrow. Just for a day or two."

"You're not serious," he said.

"I'm serious. The kid I'm looking for got snatched. I need to stage a payoff. I figure a guy like you could fix it."

Hansen laughed. His teeth were so white it made me wonder if he'd capped them to make a nice contrast to the tan and the gold necklace. "What do you think, Stash," he said, "I can just write a check?"

"What I think is you're a DEA man and the DEA is always impounding cash. Lots and lots of it. Sometimes you use that cash to set up a bust. Hell, not sometimes, most of the time."

"So? You're not talking agency involvement, are you? You're looking to bait a trap, am I right? For your own personal reasons. So where does the agency come into it?"

"I was kind of hoping the agency wouldn't have to come into it. I thought you were your own boss, more or less."

There was a float moored inside the line of buoys that marked the Pier House swimming area. A lone egret stood poised on the float, one long leg bent under a crisp white wing, motionless. Watching.

"Give me a break," Hansen said sarcastically. "You want the use of a suitcase full of loot, we have to be talking major bust, right? Everybody gets involved. Miami, D.C., everybody."

"Kurt, a kid's life is at stake."

"Uh huh. For that kind of money you can buy a boatload of kids. More kids 'n you can shake a stick at. Hell, I got Rosita for fifty a week and she lets me shake my . . . Hey, leggo my arm."

"Sorry."

"Jesus, man, that's going to bruise. What the fuck is wrong with you?"

"I'm overwrought. I didn't mean it."

"Yeah?" Hansen backed out of range without making it obvious he was in retreat. "Well, you're way out of line, cupcake. Nobody lays a hand on me."

"I guess you're not going to let me borrow a million bucks, huh?"

"You want front money, go try your buddy Zack Malone. I'm sure he's eager to help out a fellow conch. What I figure, Zach has money stashed all over the keys. Probably buried in pickle tins, which is a favorite with the rednecks." Hansen stopped rubbing where I'd grabbed him. His eyes went mean. "I'm serious, go see Malone. It can't hurt to ask, right?"

"Well," I said, "maybe a little."

Hansen still had the mean look as he pointed out a big Bertram sport fishing rig tied up to the finger pier at the hotel. A string of colored lights ran from the pulpit up to the flying bridge and down to the fighting chair in the stern. The cabin was illuminated from within. I could see the silhouettes of figures moving around inside. The bray of inebriated laughter carried across the inlet.

"Zach's having himself a birthday party," Hansen said, pinching my elbow. "I'm sure you're invited, Stash old buddy."

12

THERE was loud rock-a-billy music coming from the Bertram. Either early Conway Twitty or a Famous Floyd impersonation of him. The music sounded cheap and thin as it echoed from the concrete stacks of the hotel. A young fisherman staggered by, wearing white rubber boots and stinking of peppermint schnapps.

"Whoah, baby," he said, grabbing at the handrail. "Fucking awesome, know what I mean?"

"Sure thing."

He let go of the handrail and staggered off into the hotel shrubbery, where he collapsed with a sigh. You could just see the toes of the white rubber boots protruding from the rhododendrons.

The last time I'd dropped in on Zach Malone I had used a drunk act to get by his boys. It was unlikely to work again. Maybe what I needed was a paste-on beard or a rubber nose. "Groucho to see you, Mr. Malone, he's looking for the magic duck." Lacking a costume, or the nerve to don one, I pulled my cap down and sauntered by the party boat.

The lettering on the fat transom spelled COLLEEN in script a foot high. Someone in a vivid white T-shirt was sitting in the fighting chair, drinking from a can of beer. The cabin trunk put him in shadow, so I couldn't be sure, but he didn't look like a Malone. Behind him, at the forward end of the big cockpit, a cabin door was open. I could see heads moving by. A couple of them looked vaguely familiar, although none had the thick red hair that denoted members of the clan.

Whistling a counterpoint to the Twitty tune, I ambled along as far as the end of the pier, where the hotel tiki bar was just closing up. The shutters banged shut. The lights went off. Hotel guests fled like so many cockroaches. I leaned against the railing and remembered the .38 tucked in my waist. It would not do, I reasoned, to be carrying iron when I crashed the party.

I found a corner of the hotel complex where the spotlights didn't shine. Crouching, I wedged the revolver in a PVC drain spout. Then I stood and turned to the wall and pretended to urinate, in the off chance someone had seen me. Not much chance of that. Most anyone on the pier at that hour was in a fog of alcohol.

I went back to the *Colleen* and got to the top of the boarding ramp before the beast in the white T-shirt rose from the fighting chair to stop me.

"Who are you?" he said, blocking my way with his chest. It was a very large chest. With all the effort he'd put into making it that big, I could see why he had to keep his conversations to words of one syllable.

"Isn't it inconvenient," I asked, "walking around with no neck?"

"Huh?"

"Must be a bitch, trying to watch a tennis match. 'Scuze me," I said, attempting to squeeze by. "I promised to help Zach blow out the candles on his birthday cake."

Neckless put the flat of his hand against my breastbone, holding me in place. Gentle but firm.

"No one gets in without a name."

"Very reasonable," I said. "As it happens, I have a name."

"What is it?"

"Kilroy," I said.

"Stay," he ordered.

I'd have wagged my tail if I had one. Neckless glided over the cockpit sole and up to the cabin door, blocking the light. When he stepped down into the companionway, I crossed to the open door in time to hear Neckless say, "A Mr. Kilroy is here."

Whatever else happened, that made my night.

I ducked through the door and dropped into the companionway. What transpired next is unclear. I remember an iron band crushing my chest and the loud music going distant. Then I was in a pink canyon of pain and someone was attempting to drive a spike through the top of my head.

"Let him go," a faraway voice said. "I'll handle this."

The iron band loosened. The pinkness cleared and I was aware of Neckless propping me up on a bunk cushion. The salon was mostly oiled teak, with touches of plastic and stainless steel, and a lot of puffy red velvet cushions like the one under me. I took deep breaths and brought Zach Malone into focus. His small green eyes seemed amused. I could see four other men, one or two of whom I knew by name, and the others by reputation. Commercial fishermen who had diverted into a more lucrative line of work and who had formed a loose association under the Malone aegis. The teamsters of Florida Bay. Nary a bale of pot moved through southern waters without passing through their hands, by proxy.

"What is this, a bachelor party?" I managed to say. "Where are the girls?"

"That what you lookin' to find," Malone said, "pussy?"

He was sitting at the galley table, wearing baggy khaki trousers and a pair of new suspenders. No shirt, no shoes. There were masses of reddish hair on his chest and belly, and tufts of it on his toes. Some of the hair was going gray. I thought of a rogue male orangutan I'd once seen at a zoo, who liked to harass visitors by throwing wads of dung through the bars of his cage. When Zach raised his hand I got ready to duck.

"Give the man a drink," he said, handing one of his colleagues a bottle of Cruzan rum. "After you get your color back," he said to me, "y'all go on and tell us whatever lie you thinking up now."

I downed the rum straight from the bottle. Like a tough guy. Then I coughed like a tough guy and handed the bottle back.

"I had a pretty good fib ready for you," I said, "until it got squeezed out of my head."

"The boy don't know his own strength. Works out on one of them Nautilus machines, don't you, Earl?"

"Yes, suh," Neckless said, "I do."

"You did just fine, Earl. Now go on, get back up on deck."

Neckless went up the companionway by strength of arm, ignoring the ladder. I was impressed. My ribs were also impressed. I could feel them as I breathed, frail xylophone bones lying near to my heart.

"My associates here are of the opinion that you're some kind of narc, Mr. Kilroy. Ain't that what you're calling yourself tonight—Kilroy? Would you care to explain?"

"Explain what?" I said.

"Oh, how about starting off with something simple," Malone said, grinning slowly. "Like what you was doin' over the Annex night before last. At the DEA district office."

Malone's associates perked up. They started looking at me the way hungry men look at pork chops.

"Oh, that," I said. "That was nothing. Fishing is off, so I'm moonlighting as a custodian. You know, waxing floors?"

"Don't fun with us, son," Malone said, hooking his thumbs in the suspenders. "What'd you tell Mr. Kurt Hansen?"

"I told him if he didn't stop smoking pot, I'd report him to the President."

"This one wise-ass boy, Zach. Fire up them new diesels and let's take him for a ride, see if he can find his way home from the reef."

"See?" Malone said. "These gentlemen don't trust you, Mr. Kilroy D. Stash."

"Tell your pals to relax, Malone, I'm not here spying for Kurt Hansen or anyone else. I'm here to apply for a loan."

Malone snapped his suspenders and frowned.

"Figured it being your birthday, you'd be in a generous mood," I said.

"He's funnin' with ya, Zach."

"I'm serious," I said. "I need cash. A lot of it, and quick."

Malone stood up. As always, it was an impressive sight. He had to crane his head sideways to fit under the deck beams. The Irish Quasimodo.

"You gentlemen get some fresh air," he said. "I'm gonna have me a private word with Kilroy, here."

There was no question about whose party it was. Himself had spoken. The Florida Bay teamsters cleared out without so much as a murmur of complaint. It was obvious that they assumed Malone was going to do something so nasty he didn't want company, or witnesses, and from the evidence of sly grins, they heartily approved.

What he did, once the cabin door was bolted from

inside, was sit down at the galley table and pour us each a portion of rum.

"I knew your mother," he said, raising his glass. "A fine and gentle lady."

"That she was."

"Do me a favor, son. Tell me what the hell you're up to, and tell me straight."

So I told him. I left out the part about accessing the DEA computer, but I included most everything else. The financial woes of Famous Floyd's Palmetto Key Time-Share Resort, the boy's prideful defense of his stepfather, the stepfather's overriding concern for the boy, the mother I hadn't figured out, with her coke-wary eyes and her air of knowing more than she was letting on. When I mentioned Rey Valdez, Malone grunted.

"Damned good fisherman," he said, "for a greaser."

I told him what little I'd learned about the man who called himself Zarpa. The little girl he'd burned, his banishment from the Stock Island community, his reputation among the Mallory Dock hipsters as a rip-off artist.

"What I think happened, is he hooked up with Graham, assuming the boy had access to money. Parents live in a big house on a big estate, the old man appears on television, the obvious conclusion is that they are rich people, which they were, before they got involved in real-estate speculation. Graham must have seemed like the perfect pigeon. So Zarpa convinces the kid he can arrange a major transaction— let's say a couple of keys of cocaine. His objective is simply to rip the boy off. Take his money and deliver five pounds of sugar, or whatever is white and handy. Now, Graham is naïve, maybe, but he's not stupid. He knows if he manages to get his hands on that much cocaine, he has to find people to sell it to. He approaches local dealers, feeling them out.

Naturally, they want samples. Graham goes back to Zarpa. Zarpa finds some loser who happens to be in possession of an ounce of coke and takes it off him. What happened to the guy with the ounce, I can only guess."

"Shark bait," Malone said. He poured more rum.

"Maybe. Or maybe he got away. Or maybe it was someone else Zarpa ripped the stuff off of. It doesn't matter. What matters is that Zarpa delivers the sample, which Graham in turn cuts up and delivers to the retailers he's lining up. So far so good. Then the big deal is supposed to happen and something goes wrong. Probably a very simple thing: Graham can't get the money up."

"The mother," Malone said.

"Could be," I said. "Again, it doesn't matter. All that matters is that Zarpa is now holding the boy and making the usual demands. He's seen a few American gangster movies, I assume, and he's going for the big score. Wants a million in cash. The money or Graham's life."

"How much of this do you know?" Malone asked.

I shrugged. "I know the boy is missing. I know a phone call has been made by a Cuban. The rest is conjecture."

"And you conjecture the boy is still alive?"

"I'm hopeful."

Malone shook his massive head. The pale-green eyes seemed to bore through me. He sipped at the rum delicately, as if the fiery stuff was an aperitif. "Can't raise that kind of money on hope," he said. "That crazy Cuban'll kill the kid after he get's the dough, if he hasn't already."

"I figure that's what he plans to do."

"You're also figurin' to outsmart him, huh?"

"I'd like to give it a try."

The Malone eyes, out-of-scale small, registered

amusement. It was the look a porpoise has as it rolls in the bow wake of a boat: all power and control and sleek confidence. Turning in his seat, shifting those powerful shoulders, Malone pulled open a teak drawer under the galley counter.

I expected to see the showboat .44 emerge in his beefy fist. Instead, he gently removed a small cedar box. He set it next to the rum bottle and pried open the lid with his thumb.

"The real McCoy," he said, handing me a cigar. "The exact same ones they make for old Fidel. Rolled from one leaf."

Malone expected me to smoke with him, so I did. He clipped the one end with a little gadget he kept in the cedar box and warmed the other with a wooden match before firing it up. I mimicked him, doing my best not to inhale. I am no tobacco expert, but it was a damn good smoke, as strong and heady in its way as fine marijuana, and it worked like that for Malone, relaxing him in a way the rum had not.

The big man began to talk. By no means eloquent, he was nevertheless able to spin a yarn, like most fishermen. His subject, for the most part, was old Key West. The good old days before the wealthy gays and the tourists and the developers conspired to manufacture legal prosperity. The wrecking days, when wealth was measured in doubloons and silver candlesticks rowed in from the reef. The glory time before the great hurricane tore away Flagler's railway.

"I was five years old when that storm come ashore. My daddy had us all out on the roof of that little dirt-floor cabin we lived in. Had his boat lashed to the ridge post. They was eight feet of mean seas washing over the island, son, and the wind was liftin' rooftops like a gentleman tippin' his hat. Was ten thousand living on the island then, and six hundred of 'em drowned. Rolled through the streets like

logs. Well, what happened, the water went back
down, but that was the beginning of hard times.
Daddy's boat got smashed all to hell. Which didn't
make a lot of difference 'cause this was the Great
Depression, son, and you couldn't get a dime a
bushel for fish, nor for crabs nor crawdaddies neither. Without his boat, though, Daddy lost his pride.
Never drew a sober breath till the day he died, so it
was on me to see we had enough to eat so our bones
didn't show through. They call it malnutrition now,
but in them days most everyone in Key West was
half-starved. Stayed bad until the war came and they
built that navy base."

"Sigsbee," I said, thinking of my father.

"Best thing every happen to this island," Malone
said, rolling the cigar in his sausage fingers. "World
War Two. God bless the krauts. I was fifteen years
old when they dropped the bomb and ended the
thing, and you better believe I was severely disappointed."

"You wanted to be a hero."

"Exactly right," he said, nodding. "That's a thing
most men grow out of, wanting to be a hero. Take it
from me, son, a hero is almost always a damned
fool."

The cigar was making me dizzy. Or maybe it was
the rum. I didn't cotton immediately to the point
Malone was making about heroes and fools.

"The other thing heroes mostly are," he said, leaning close enough so I could smell Castro on his
breath, "is dead."

It was a warning, not a threat. I responded by
explaining that I was looking for a wayward son, not
a medal, and that it was impossible to do anything
of value without taking some risk. Heroes, I agreed,
were mostly fools.

"My question," he said. "What you gonna do,

you don't find no money to set up whatever crazy scheme you got in mind?"

I shrugged. "Cut up newspapers, I guess, and pack 'em in a suitcase. Anything to fake it, get close enough."

Malone put the cigar down and looked at the rum bottle for a while. He made no move to pour from it. I could almost hear his thoughts ticking over. He seemed to be waiting for something, or someone, and I didn't dare break the mood.

There was a knock on the cabin door. Malone stood up, expressionless. When he slipped back the latch I could see that the stars had faded. The salty scent of morning mixed with the pong of cigar smoke. Malone spoke quietly with someone on deck—I never did know who it was. When he turned back to me, his face was no longer blank.

"You're clear, son," he said with a Chiclet's grin.

"Clear?" I didn't have to fake confusion.

He settled back in his seat and nodded, stifling a yawn. "My boys are back," he said.

The light breaking through the portholes seemed to clear the fog from my brain. His boys were back. Now it made sense. The rum, the tales of old Key West, the genuine Cuban cigars, it had all been part of an effort to keep me there aboard *Colleen* while his sons were out working. That was why none of them had been there to help the old man celebrate his birthday. They were giving him a bigger present. Running home with a motherlode.

Malone didn't tell me that, of course. He didn't need to. The grin said it all. He'd been keeping me hostage to the fate of his children. If Hansen had managed to bust the Malone clan that night, my complicity would have been proven, in Zach's small green eyes.

"You look a little gray around the gills, Kilroy."

"I feel like my horse just won the race, but I forgot to make the bet. Because I never knew there *was* a race, know what I mean?"

"I think I do, son. Tell you what I'm gonna do, seein' as how I'm in a generous mood. I'm gonna tell you where to find what you're looking for."

I sat up straight. "Graham?"

"Nah," he said. "Not the boy. The money you need to cut him loose."

"A million?" I said hopefully.

"More or less. I never did bother counting it, and prob'bly the trap rats have et some it by now, but there oughta be enough left," he said, "to fool a dumb shit Marielito."

13

WHAT I wanted most in the world was to go home, take the phone off the hook, pull the shades, and sleep. Instead I drove out to Palmetto Key. The breeze through the missing windshield helped keep me awake. The sun was rising directly behind the Chilly estate. In the low slant of light the lawns were pink and the gravel in the driveway glinted like diamonds on the road to Oz.

There was a new security guard at the gate. He flashed a thumbs-up and waved me through before I could explain. Evidently my reputation had preceded me, or he'd been warned to expect a funky Cadillac.

Floyd was waiting in the parking area. His eyes were weary and bloodshot. The pencil-thin mustache was getting blurred and his color was bad. When he reached out to pull my door open, his hands were trembling.

"I been callin' y'all for hours," he said. "We heard from Graham."

There was fear in those watery blue eyes, and the baritone voice was breaking down, like a speaker with a bad connection. I insisted that he sit down on the front steps and catch his breath.

"I got it on tape, like you wanted. He sounded scared. I mean really scared. Reggie went off her head after the call. I had to get a doctor. He give her a shot of something and she's dead to the world, so I been keeping watch, just in case he calls again."

Insisting that he was okay, Floyd hauled himself back to his feet and then sat down suddenly.

"Hell," he whispered. "I think my pins give out. I'll just set here a minute, y'all go in ahead."

Carlos, the original security guard, was in the main house, where he had volunteered to stay for the duration, to act as translator should he be needed. Out of uniform, wearing a guayabera shirt, chinos, and sandals, he looked even younger than I had remembered. He was strong enough, though, to help me carry Floyd up the stairs and into the living room.

"I feel like a silly old puppet," Floyd apologized as we put him on a couch, "like somebody cut my strings."

"Can you feel your legs?"

He nodded. "Feel 'em fine. They just too weak to work proper."

"We better get the doctor back here and have him check you out."

"Later. First I want you to listen to that tape. Then I want you to tell me what the hell we gonna do to get the boy away. That crazy bastard is damn sure hurtin' him."

The cassette recorder was on the bar top, where I'd wired it up to the gaudy pink telephone. Floyd watched intently from the couch, his face sagging under the effort to keep awake, to concentrate. I pushed the PLAY button and listened.

"It's me, Daddy" it began. "I really fucked up."

A Spanish-inflected voice hissed in the background. There was a banging sound, possibly a phone-booth door bumping shut.

"De prisa," the Spanish voice shouted. *"Rápido! Rápido!"*

"I gotta hurry, Dad. He cut me a little b-b-but I'm okay. Just a scratch, really. Tell Mom I'm sorry, really sorry. Tell her it was all a big mistake."

"Dinero, tonto. Esta noche!"

"He wants the money, Dad. I told him no way, but he says tonight, or he's gonna cut me b-b-bad."

There was a thud, a groan, a muffled cry.

"Esta noche, tonight" the voice said, breathing hard into the phone. *"Un millón*, okay fine. *A las diez de la noche."*

The line went dead. I reversed the tape and played it through again, stopping and starting, trying to pick up anything significant in the background. In the movies there is always some clue, a train whistle, a cash register, a particular tune on a jukebox. All I could hear was a stuttering, terrified boy pleading for his life. I shut off the recorder, making sure it was ready to roll for the next call, if it came.

From the couch, Floyd's voice sounded hollow, utterly defeated. "What am I gonna do?" he asked. "How am I gonna find a million bucks by ten tonight? You heard him. He's gonna kill the boy, we don't pay him the money."

I told him, briefly and without naming names, about the deal I'd made with Zach Malone. You could see it in the old troubadour's face, like something lifting to an incoming tide. Hope flooding back in.

"Oh, man," he sighed. "That's beautiful. That's good. You think it will work?"

"No promises, Mr. Chilly. If it's dark enough, he may fall for it. I figure I need about ten, fifteen seconds to get the drop on him. With any luck, the stuff will fool him for that long."

"And if it don't?"

I shrugged. "I'll just have to wait and see. You go into something like this with too many preconceived notions, you don't react quick enough when the time comes."

"You really think it'll work. You'll get Graham back okay?"

"I'll give it my best shot," I said. "Understand, this is no typical kidnapper we're dealing with. It didn't start out as a snatch, and the guy who's got Graham is not playing by anyone's rules."

I left it at that. No point in mentioning my conviction that time was running out, that the chance of Graham surviving much longer in the company of Zarpa was slim indeed. There was more than enough corroboration of the reports of Zarpa's behavior to suggest that he was accustomed to instant gratification. Whatever didn't please him died. Or maybe it was the dying that pleased him.

Floyd was insistent about not wanting the doctor back. I found Carlos in the kitchen, reading the *Miami Herald.* Somebody had given him an exaggerated version of my qualifications because he was deferential to a degree that made me uncomfortable. He seemed to think that a good word from T. D. Stash would get him on the list for a state police job. I didn't have enough energy to dissuade him.

"You need extra hands," he said earnestly. "I am ready to assist."

"I think about it," I said. "Right now I need help getting Mr. Chilly into bed. He's at the point of nervous collapse. I want him to get some sleep."

It was no great surprise to learn that Floyd and Reggie had separate bedrooms. Floyd's was a suite, really, adjoined by what he called his trophy room. He had an expensive, built-in stereo system, a collection of several thousand record albums arranged by artist and category, three guitars perched on stands, and a wall of framed pictures of himself as Famous Floyd in various publicity stills. He was grinning in all of the pictures—an expression he hadn't had much use for lately. A gold record of his *Greatest Hits*, the order-by-phone album, was at eye level in the center of the wall. Nowhere on the record or the presentation plaque was there any mention of the fact that he was singing other artist's greatest hits, not his own. All part of the sales strategy, no doubt. Near the gold record was a wedding picture. Reggie in a slinky yellow gown, holding a bouquet of flowers. Graham was beside his mother, wearing a sky-blue tuxedo that matched the one Floyd had on. Of the three, the boy looked to be the happiest. A kid's toothy, excited smile. You could see where he was gripping his mother's arm harder than he intended.

When I turned back to the adjoining bedroom, Floyd was sitting on the edge of the king-sized bed, stripped down to his boxer shorts. Carlos was standing in front of him, holding a thick book in his hands. A bible.

"You don't worry about nothing, Mr. Chilly," the guard was saying. "I no leave this house."

"That makes me feel real good, kid. Now jess go on ahead and swear it on that holy bible. May you be struck with a pox if you leave the house or fail to answer the phone."

Carlos honored the request, his shoulders at attention, back ramrod-straight. He would make, one of these days, an exemplary trooper.

"You're a good egg," Floyd said, easing himself down on the pillows. "He's a good egg, ain't he, Stash?"

"An egg?" the young Cuban said. "What is it to be an egg?"

"It's good," I said. "Take my word for it. Now go on out there and do your duty."

He marched out, resolute and baby-faced. I sat

down next to the bed and promised Floyd that I
would have Graham back in one piece in less than
twenty-four hours. He didn't ask me to swear it on
the bible and I didn't offer. It was the kind of promise you make to a man about to surrender to despair,
without any real certainty of keeping it.

"You know what I almost did today?" he said,
staring at the overhead fan. "I almost took a drink."

"But you didn't."

"It was a close thing. Had it all poured out and up
to my lips. I don't think Reggie even noticed. I think
that was what gave me the strength to put it back
down, knowing she wouldn't even have noticed."

There was nothing to say to that. I was exhausted,
empty inside. As I got up to leave, Floyd spoke with
his eyes closed, "She was in it with the boy," he
said. "I guess I knew all along. Damn-fool notion of
getting a quick cash turnover to impress our creditors."

"Reggie?"

He nodded. "Don't make no difference now. She
and Graham just picked the wrong deal, I guess. It
was wrongheaded from the start, which is why they
tried to keep it from me. This real-estate thing has
been a great burden to her, Stash. It was her idea
and she just can't let go of it. I tol' her; I said,
Honey, I been broke before. Ain't no big deal. We'll
let the house go to the creditors and we'll go back on
the road, the three of us. Reggie can book me into
the clubs and Graham can be road manager. Hell, I
can still clear a couple thousand a week doing gigs.
That ain't bad. Heck, it might even be fun. With that
and the royalties from the *Greatest Hits* we can build
a nest egg back up in a year or two. It ain't like we'd
be poor. Far from it."

He mumbled on as I took my leave, about how
good it would be, just the three of them on tour
again, living out of a luxury bus he figured to lease.

Maybe he'd hire Carlos to drive, the young man seemed clearheaded enough.

"That little bus'd be cozy," he said. "Folks tend to get close, living on the road. It'd be a good thing for us, we just give up on what we had going here and hit the road."

I don't think he believed in the possiblility of the fantasy coming true. He was imagining sheep with golden fleece, counting them as they leapt the broken stiles of his dreams.

Ten at night. If Zarpa made the call then, as he had threatened, there was a little less than twelve hours remaining. Somehow I had to find time to ready the payoff, conceive a strategy that would leave me alive after payment was surrendered, and catch a few hours' sleep. Since I was having trouble marshaling coherent thoughts, the strategy-conception part would have to wait on sleep.

I was about to turn into my yard when I remembered that I'd forgotten to retrieve the .38 from the rain gutter at Pier House. For a moment I considered leaving it there until I'd slept and showered. Then I thought about the children at the resort, and how the downspout would be at eye level for a five-year old, and I swung wide of the driveway and headed for the waterfront. The Conch Train was stalled on Front Street, backing up traffic. Passengers were getting out of the open cars, clutching string bags of shells and knick-knacks and tying up the whole street. I hadn't the energy to honk the horn, although no one else was shy about making noise.

In my head a sluggish clock was ticking. I wedged the coupe into a space, blocking a hydrant, and got out. No point in locking up. Some people chase rainbows—T. D. Stash was chasing windshields, and not getting close to one, either. In the trunk I found a torn canvas tool bag full of rusty wrenchs. With the bag clanking at my side I could pass for a typical Key West repairman, hung over and dazed and not entirely certain, man, what hotel had called about the leaky gutter.

Colleen was no longer at the dock where Malone had hosted his little party. In her place was a harbor tour boat about a third full of sunburned tourists. Take away their sunglasses and they looked like steamed lobsters on a deep serving platter. Not a fair comparison, maybe, since most everyone gets to be a tourist someday, but I tend to make snap judgments when I don't get my beauty rest.

The gun was where I'd left it. I tapped the drainspout until it came loose and caught it in the canvas bag. An unnecessary precaution, as it turned out. No one noticed. For all the attention I attracted, I could have put the pistol in a holster and walked bowlegged down Duval Street, rattling my spurs.

When I got back to the coupe a traffic cop was trying to figure where to put the ticket.

"This is a new one on me," she said. "Usually it goes on the windshield."

"I'm a plumber," I said, holding up the canvas tool bag. "Emergency call at the Pier House."

"You're a plumber, huh? You ever do small jobs, like fixing the leak under my kitchen sink?"

"Strictly commercial," I said.

"Fine," she said, handing me the ticket. "Stick this in your pocket. And have a nice day."

I thought of a snappy comeback about twenty minutes later. By then I was lying on my back in a darkened bedroom, lulled by the faint wheezing noise of the air-conditioner. I never did drop soundly off. Drifting near the edge, I would get to the point where I was almost ready to fall over, but something intangible would draw me back. Now and then the air-conditioner seemed to transmit distant voices from a dream I couldn't quite enter. The plaintive sound of a badly frightened boy: "Tell Mom I'm sorry, really sorry." Then there was the snake-rattle voice of a man who burned little girls with matches, and the broken baritone of a Southern gentleman. After a while they all began to mix together, a chorus without music. When the alarm went off at two in the afternoon, I sat up and put my bare feet on the cool tile floor and thought, No one can make you have a nice day.

14

I was hunched over a late breakfast at El Cacique when someone called my name. I put the coffee mug down, swiveled the stool, and saw a blonde with hair done in thick, ropy braids. She wore a strapless pink sundress with matching pink sunglasses.

"Trudy," I said, "I didn't recognize you."

"Never seen me in a dress, huh?" She laughed, tipped the shades up on her head.

"About Smathers Beach," I began.

"Something came up," she finished. "You couldn't make it."

"Right. It was that missing kid, Graham. I had to—"

"Skip it," Trudy said, grinning. "It's fine. I don't mind."

"You don't?" I said uncertainly.

She shook her head, causing the yellow braids to flop against her fine brown shoulders. "No." She laughed. "It's cool. It's great. What happened is I met this guy Duane, we went to high school together?"

"In Nebraska?"

"Sure, in Nebraska. I went over to the beach when I got off work, like we agreed, and waited awhile for you. Then I figure, Well, the guy is on a job, he's working, I'll go by his house and see what exactly happened, he couldn't meet me at the beach, which he promised come hell or high water, I think it was?"

"Yup," I said. "My exact words."

"So I was on my way over to your house when I happened to walk by this guy sitting on the seawall, right? I mean it was like something out of a movie, Stash. This guy used to sit behind me in biology and copy my answers and then somehow ten years go by and he's sitting on a seawall in Key West."

"And now you're getting on like a house afire."

Trudy looked puzzled. Maybe a little disappointed I wasn't able to share her giddy excitement about Duane from Nebraska. "Well, I wouldn't put it that way, exactly. But you get the idea. Duane is a professor now. He's down here doing research on Tennessee Williams, and it's just the most incredible coincidence we happened to meet out there at Smathers Beach."

"Under the moon and stars."

"Yeah." The cornflower-blue eyes made an appeal. "Come on, T.D., be a pal. Be happy for me."

There's no easy way to resist a woman in love, even when she's not in love with you, and so I said of course I would be a pal and that of course I was happy for her. As I was leaving Duane returned from the men's room. As blond and corn-fed as Trudy, with a bright, easy smile and a firm handshake. Said he was pleased to meet me, and sounded like he meant it.

"You don't look like a professor," I said.

"Well," he said, winking at Trudy, "it's hard to put elbow patches on a short-sleeve shirt."

The wink was chock full of encoded information about how he knew about me sleeping with Trudy and how he wasn't threatened by that fact, and how I had reacted in character by inadvertently insulting his profession, which insult he had deflected in good humor, thereby claiming victory in the field of love. Whew. I gathered up my broken lance and my shattered shield and my go-cup of coffee, and went.

You already know about not eating at a place named Mom's and not playing poker with a man called Doc. Here's another piece of advice: never get in a winking contest with a guy named Duane.

The trap yard Zach Malone sent me to was on a built-up mangrove swamp on the southside of Boca Chica Key, four miles east of Key West. Not all of Malone's business was illegitimate. He and various members of his horde fished stone crab and crawfish in season, and he had leased the former mangrove swamp to store the traps, since Key West waterfront was at a premium. There was a chain-link fence surrounding the storage area, and the gate, as he'd promised, was broken. I walked it open, drove the coupe through, and pushed it shut.

As olfactory experiences went, the yard was powerful and varied. Salt air, creosote, rotting baitfish, ammoniated gull shit, and under it all the corpse stench of the buried mangroves. The traps were stacked six high, in a maze of rows. There were no palms, no shade to relieve the furnace blast of sunlight, nothing but crab traps and craw traps and strings of painted buoys.

I parked the coupe where it couldn't be seen from the road and tried to get my bearings. East of the hill, Malone had said. The hill, in fishing parlance, is the place where the traps are repaired and dipped. I found a collection of creosote drums and a chainfalls rigged from a cedar gallows post, and faced east.

Seventh row from the hill, Malone has said. Just remember lucky seven. Over rum and cigars on the *Colleen* it had sounded simple, a piece of cake. In the yard, with the sun beating down, the stacks and rows of traps did not fit the picture in my head. Which seventh row, for instance, the one to the right or the one to the left?

I tried the right row first and found it wrong. Dead-ended, Malone had promised, and it wasn't. I cut back, tripping over the rough chunks of limestone that had been bulldozed as fill, and tried the row to the left. A stack of traps blocked the end. So far so good.

"Can't recall what trap, exactly," Malone had said with a lying smile, " 'cept it's near to the ground and a little ways back from the end." As if he had stashed a bag of counterfeit fifties and neglected to note the precise location. Malone knew, I was certain of that; he just wanted the pleasure of knowing I'd have to root through his fetid, and as it turned out, infested crab traps.

Down on my hands and knees, squinting into the creosote-stained netting along the bottom row, I found a pair of small black eyes looking back at me.

"Rats!"

It wasn't a casual exclamation. Indeed, there were rats. Large rats. Bold rats. Rats grown fat on baitfish and bird eggs. Rats who patrolled the traps as if they were deeded tenants in rat-dominiums.

I have no particular animus against rodents but I wasn't real enthusiastic about reaching into the traps and risking a bite. So I developed an early-warning technique. This involved beating the slats with a length of two-by-four and making catlike sounds. No doubt my rodent friends were insulted, but they did temporarily vacate the area.

After an hour of trap-bashing and cat-hissing I was about ready to give it up, convinced there was no plastic garbage bag of bogus bills on the premises. Zach Malone had been funning with me. Wearily, knees aching from the sharp-edged limestone scrabble, I flailed at one last row of traps. And there, fluttering right in front of my nose, was a piece of green and gray paper. It was the torn-off corner of a fifty-dollar bill, and it rekindled my limited faith in Zachary C. Malone.

I peered into the bottom trap. With my cheek hugging the ground, I saw a glint of dull light. Not, from the unblinking steadiness of it, an animal. Using a broken-off slat, I poked at it. The glint was from a black plastic surface.

"Come to Poppa," I whispered, working my hand into the parlor of the trap. The plastic was slippery. Small tear holes were evident, tooth-sized. When I finally worked the whole bag to the mouth of the trap, I half-expected to find the bills chewed up into so much useless green confetti.

Dropping the broken slat, I pulled the bag loose with both hands. Banded stacks of bills poured forth. Fifties, as green as a seasick snowbird. Some of the edges were chewed, but not badly. Evidently the printing job was so dreadful not even the rats were fooled.

It was the color that ruined the pretty illusion of wealth. The counterfeiter that had cranked out that particular batch must have been high on ink fumes, because the green was *too* green. Chartreuse funny money, easily spotted as bogus from across the street. How exactly they had come into Malone's possession was not something he had chosen to confide. The best guess was that someone had tried to pull a fast one during a payoff, and Zach had kept the worthless batch for sentimental reasons, or because he hadn't yet figured a way to pass them along to the next sucker.

That is, until T. D. Stash came begging. I tossed the bundles back in the bag, made two ears of the plastic ends, and tied it, treating the stuff like the garbage it was. I'd told Floyd Chilly all I needed to do was fool Zarpa for eight or ten seconds, just long enough to distract him. After seeing the stuff I decided to pray for a moonless night and hope that the Marielito was color-blind, it was that bad.

I heard the pickup truck come into the yard, engine gunning, before I saw it. Dropping the plastic bag, I clambered up on a trap and peeped over the top of the stacks. The top of the truck cab was visible as it circled the storage area at high speed. There was a rack of lights on top and a whip antenna. The driver was visible only in flashes as the truck passed openings in the rows of stacks. I could see just enough of him to make me think he might be a Malone. Since I was on family territory, it made sense.

Had Daddy sent him? Was I being set up? Or was the driver merely getting his rocks off skidding the jacked-up truck around the trap yard? I trusted Malone about as far as I could throw his Cuban cigars. Keeping my head low, I was able to peer through the slats, following the vehicle's progress. It slowed at about the area where I'd left the coupe, then speeded up again before coming to an abrupt halt on the opposite side of the yard, roughly parallel with the row where I was hiding. A door slammed. There was a glimpse of red brush-cut, then the door slammed again and the truck streaked away. It stopped just outside the gate and I heard the faint clashing sound of the gate door being shut. Out on the blacktop there was a screech of burning rubber and then, finally, silence.

Checking me out, apparently. Taking the mysterious visitation as a cue to leave, I gathered up the bulky plastic sack of cash. At first I thought the scrabbling sound was me, kicking rocks as I trudged along with the bag. I stopped and the scabbling sound continued. It got louder. Fast skitterings, like something running low and fast. I was turning to look when it hit me, tearing into my ankle.

There are dog lovers out there who like pit bulls, who claim their murderous reputation is exaggerated. Probably they have never been hit by one charging at full speed. In that first moment, before the pain started, I had no idea why my legs were going out from under me. I landed flat on my back and rolled over.

The force of its charge carried the dog past me. It hit a stack of traps, flipping over as its legs dug furiously into the loose limestone. The dog looked to be all teeth, a small slavering pair of locomotive jaws. The lips were curled back and the eyes, set in folds of loose skin, blinked furiously as it struggled to regain momentum.

I was back on my feet before I quite knew what was going on. The pain began to resonate from my torn ankle, a thrum of hot agony. The pit bull charged again, its powerful chest low to the ground. I swung the bulky bag. The mass of it threw the dog off target and it crashed violently into another stack of traps, evidently unhurt and obviously furious. I grabbed a crab trap and hurled it. The end hit the ground and the trap rolled. The dog twisted out of the way, jaws snapping.

If there had been a palm tree on the property I'd have been up it instantly, bad ankle and all. The best I could do was scramble to the top of a stack of traps, knocking half of them over in the process. The tumbling traps slowed the pit bull down, and possibly whetted his appetite. I lay across the top of the uneven stack, the bag of cash under me, and felt the beast smashing into the lower traps in a rage.

Tucked in the waist of my jeans was the .38 Nelson Kerry had suggested I carry. He had psychopaths in mind, not pit bulls, but a bullet between the eyes would have the same effect, regardless of the species. Before I thought about shooting the dog, however, I needed to attend to the ankle the thing had attempted to shred. My sneaker was full of blood and more of it was pouring out with each beat of my pulse.

I twisted out of my shirt and tried to wrap it tight around the lower part of my calf. My eyes flooded with tears and my ears popped, as if adjusting for a new and higher atmosphere. The thrum of pain started matching itself to my pulse. I could hear the pit bull making vain attempts to climb the side of the traps.

The bleeding slowed to a steady drip. I told myself the faint-headedness I felt was a result of the pain, not of blood loss. I lay back on the bag and thought about the absurdity of having hundreds of thousands of bogus dollars as the stuffing for my pillow. After a few deep breaths I could feel my pulse beginning to slow.

After getting a handle on the pain I sat up and pulled the .38 out. With one arm locked firmly over the traps, I leaned out with the gun. The dog saw me and began to bark.

It was the barking that saved its life. Yapping, it sounded like any other dog, and not a particularly big one at that. I drew a bead on its head, aiming at the snapping jaws, and thought about making it shut up forever. Then I thought about Zach Malone and the redhead spawn of his who had sicced the beast on me, and my finger relaxed on the trigger. One-hundred-and-eighty-five-pound man blows away thirty-pound canine with an ounce of lead—there was a descending order of mass there that made me consider alternate methods of escape.

Standing up on the wobbly traps was precarious. The pit bull, who I had begun to think of as Jaws, followed on the ground, barking frantically. Every few yards it would launch itself in a futile attack, slamming into the stacks. From on high I was able to discern a sort of pattern in the maze of stacks, and slowly worked toward the coupe.

Jaws was tireless. It would bark, snap, attack, then back off and race around to the other side of whatever particular stack I was traversing. The ankle continued to bleed some. The pain was reduced to a constant throb. I limped over the tops of the traps, dragging the bag of funny money, trading insults with Jaws, who barked a good game.

Getting down to the car was the tricky part. I'd parked it between two stacks, with about a yard of clearance. Jaws, as if sensing my imminent escape, went wild. I hefted the bag of loot and tossed it down into the back seat. A couple of loose fifties drifted up like autumn leaves. Jaws snapped at one, impaling the bill on a lower tooth before tearing it to shreds with his front paws.

Next I tossed the .38 onto the front seat. The idea of having it in my waist when I jumped was troublesome. I was willing to lose my pound of flesh, but there were those few private ounces that were sacred to me.

I jumped, made dumb little-birdie motions with my arms, and crashed into the big back seat. Deprived of adequate running room to make a leap over the door, Jaws concentrated on trying to scratch his way up the side of the car. When I got my breath back I crawled over the seat and got behind the wheel. The keys were in the ignition.

"First try," I said to the coupe. "Pretty please? Poppa will get you a new windshield, promise."

It started. I popped into gear, half-hoping Jaws would be under the wheels. A new, desperate tone to the scratching sound made me glance in the rearview mirror as I pulled out. The dog had somehow got leverage at the bumper and was actually scampering up over the trunk.

I put the pedal to the metal and Jaws slid off, tumbling as he fell. This was one determined pit bull. It chased the Caddy through the storage yard and kept on coming after I popped open the front gate with the front bumper. Legs a furious blur, the dog didn't begin to fade from sight until I was a mile or so down Boca Chica Road.

It took seven stitches to close the gash on my ankle. Lucky seven. The doctor who sewed me up said I might want to think about rabies shots. I said there were a few people I wanted to bite, if it came to that. The doctor said, Oh, and gave me Darvon for the pain and a prescription for antibiotics. To him I was just another crazy conch fisherman. For all he knew I'd chawed up the ankle myself.

At home I put the Darvon away, substituting black coffee with a shot of Irish whiskey. While that was working I dialed the Chilly number. Carlos answered.

"Any word from our Marielito friend?" I asked.

"No. The lady is in with Mr. Floyd now," he said quietly. "She is crying again, I think. They are both very nervous-acting."

"They've a right to be," I said. "Tell them I've got the money. I'll be there by eight and we'll wait for the call together. Got that?"

He repeated the message.

"You're doing fine, Carlos. No matter how 'nervous-acting' they get, you just be cool, okay? I need a level head in the house."

"Sure, okay."

"I'll see you all in a few hours."

There are times when whiskey and caffeine are usefully combined. I decided that one Irish coffee every hour was the proper dosage, and then set about the business of preparing the money. The first thing I did was select one of the several old suitcases cluttering up the attic. There was a square-edged, hard-sided number with a big brass snap lock that would do nicely. The second thing I did was strip the mattress from my bed. I needed s spring device and the easiest way to get it was to clip a couple of coils out of the box spring. That would be two things the Floyd Chilly owed me: the *Golden Oldie* and a new box spring.

I attached the spring coils to the inside of the suitcase with plenty of duct tape and tried them out. Nice action. Next I cut out a section of corrugated cardboard that was slightly smaller than the inside of the suitcase and put that atop the springs.

Then came the fun part. Stacking money. Twenty-five hundred in each bundle. I stopped counting after a while. It didn't matter if there was a million, because by the time Zarpa counted it he would know it was counterfeit. I didn't intend for him to count it. What was supposed to happen, he would pop open the latch to see the money and the springs would make the stacks of bills spill out. He would reach for the loot, attempting to gather it up. He would do this because it is the natural, human reaction in the presence of what looks like a great sum of money, to take it up by the handful.

That was supposed to be my edge. While Zarpa was distracted by the spilling money, I would get the drop on him. I would shoot him if it seemed like a good idea. I would not kill him if at all possible because I did not like to kill things, not even a man who burned little girls with matches.

That was my plan.

15

THE neon flamingo was flapping its crippled wing as I came down the long curve of the driveway. Somehow or other I had missed seeing it on my previous visits to Palmetto Key. That night, arriving with a suitcase of chartreuse money and high hopes, the pink flamingo beckoned from a reflecting pool on Famous Floyd's estate. The bird was one of Reggie's design motifs for the resort, I later learned. Instead of the usual dime-store plastic, she'd had the flamingo made of bent neon tubes, with a single wing that appeared to flap as the light switched on and off. There by transforming the tacky folk symbol of Florida into a chic new icon.

The time-share resort was about to go belly-up, but the hot-pink bird flapped on, pinned to the earth, as pretty and fragile as romance. I skidded the coupe through the white gravel chips and got out, leaving the suitcase in the trunk.

Carlos opened the door, obviously relieved to see me. "The lady has been drinking," he warned.

Reggie glided over, wearing tight black jeans and a satin blouse the color of ripe peaches, and kissed me on the mouth. She smelled of gin and orange blossoms.

"Enter the hero," she said thickly.

"How's Floyd?"

"Floyd," she said, with a faint air of disdain, "is his usual self."

"He was having trouble with his legs."

She slipped her arm in mine as we descended into the sunken living room. "He's made a miraculous recovery," she said. "He walks, he talks, he waits by the telephone. Now you're the one who's limping."

"I stepped in something," I said. "It bit me."

Floyd had shaved and showered and his eyes were clear. He was sitting on a hassock next to a glass coffee table, smoking a cigarette. On the table, casting a faint reflection in the glass, was the ugly pink telephone.

"Darling," Reggie said with a theatrical trill, "our redeemer cometh."

Floyd snubbed the cigarette out. Slicked back, his hair looked as thin as black lacquer. There were new lines in his face, and a gray pallor under the fading tan. "Pay her no attention," he said. "It's the medication she's taking, makes her talk like that."

"If you say so, dear," Reggie said, plopping on a couch and patting the space next to her. "I say it's the gin. Or the air. Don't you find it muggy this evening, T.D.? And who was it bit your poor little ankle?"

"A four-legged shark," I said. "Could I get a coffee?"

Reggie laughed. It sounded like breaking glass. "If you can get a million dollars," she said, "you can certainly get a cup of coffee. Carlos, get Mr. Stash a cup of coffee."

"He's not a houseboy," I said.

"Oh? Well, pardon me, but if he's in the house he *must* be a houseboy, mustn't he?"

"Reggie, please," Floyd said. "She's jagged up on them pills the doctor give her. I told her you ain't supposed to mix booze and pills, but she went ahead."

Reggie made a face and pointed at her husband. "He knows all about booze and pills, that one."

"Damn right," he said. "I surely do."

Carlos arrived with a mug of coffee. In a grave undertone he assured me he was keeping cool, exactly as I had requested. I added a dose of whiskey and drank it down.

Reggie patted the place next to her again and said, "Come on and sit down, handsome. Take a load off your feet. Your foot. Floyd doesn't mind if you sit next to me, do you, Floyd?"

"No," he said wearily. "I don't mind nothing."

As social calls went, it was a humdinger. Whatever she was on—be it gin or pills or cocaine—Reggie had achieved a low, unstable orbit. She would loop out, facing the sun, all smiles, talking in a loosely assembled flock of words. Then, as gravity pulled her around to the dark side, her eyes would go dead and the irritating bird chatter would stop. The British accent waxed and waned with the cycle. Sometimes she was a Southern belle, sometimes she was Dame Regina, fluting droll comments through an upturned nose.

I didn't know how to turn her off and Floyd had plainly given up trying. We sat like two refugees from an Albee play, waiting for the phone to ring. During one of her dark, quiet moods Floyd suggested that he and I take a stroll out to the dock. We left Reggie staring at her fingernails and went down the back steps to the patio, and from there to the pier where the *Golden Oldie* was tied up. Floyd made no comment about my new limp or the gauze bandages around my ankle. I'm not sure he even noticed.

"I been meaning to sign over the bill of sale," he said, resting a hand on the rub rail. "You earned her, even if we don't get the boy back safe."

"I'll get him back," I said. "That was the deal."

"We both know what can happen to deals," he said, nodding toward the main house.

The documentation for the boat was in a water-proof file in the wheelhouse. He insisted I sit at the chart table while he signed the registration over to me. The boat, he said, was still under warranty. There were less than thirty hours on the engines and the bottom paint was good for another season.

"When I ordered the thing built I figured me and the boy would go on overnighters. Out to the Marquesas, maybe. By the time I took delivery on her Graham had developed other interests. We fished Kingfish Shoals just the one time. Then it seemed like the development sort of swallowed up every spare hour and I hardly give the boat a thought. You aim to sell her?"

I nodded. I still had my heart set on that pretty little Herreshoff ketch. "If things work out, maybe I'll sell her back to you."

"That's an idea," Floyd said. "If things work out."

Reggie had the stereo cranked up when we returned. A Leon Russell tune, "Back to the Island." She took hold of my hands and wouldn't let go until I danced with her, waltzing against the soft, clutching friction of the carpet. Pressing the swell of her breasts against me, her fist tight in the small of my back. There was nothing sensual about it. More like she was clinging to a handy spar in a storm.

Floyd paid no attention. He was fully occupied watching the clock and the telephone.

"I know you hate me," Reggie whispered in a sultry voice. "You think this is all my fault."

"Isn't it?" I stopped dancing and extricated myself from her grip.

"I had no idea," she said, her face beginning to fragment. "No idea. It didn't seem real, that kind of money."

"It wasn't."

"You *hate* me. You think I'm a horrible mother."

I made her sit down. "I don't hate anybody," I said.

We waited until it was ten o'clock, *las diez de la noche*, and then we waited some more. Reggie wore the Leon Russell song out. When it got to the end she would punch the REPLAY button and we were back to the islands again, with the drifting guitar and the Caribbean rhythm. Reggie danced alone, hand splayed at her waist, arm cocked for an invisible partner. She tried to coax Carlos into joining her. Mortified, he retreated to the kitchen.

At ten-fifteen Reggie capitulated to her husband's demands and turned off the stereo. She poured herself what aficionados of the drink call a dry martini; what the unenamored call a simple glass of gin.

"It's not going to happen," Floyd said, clenching his blocky fists. "Something has gone wrong."

At ten-twenty-six the phone rang. As her husband reached for the receiver, Reggie seemed to shrink into the couch, like a flower closing its petals. Floyd put the phone to his ear, looked at me, and nodded.

"We have your money ready," he spoke into the mouthpiece. "Give us our boy."

I can't swear that someone tailed me from the Boca Chica bridge. In a rearview mirror, headlights tend to blur and the backlit silhouette of one sedan is very like another. It was just a feeling that settled on the back of my neck, a cross-hair itch that made me wish I was driving an armored tank rather than a ragtop Cadillac with taillights as big and bright as rocket fins.

It wasn't the uncertainty of walking into a trap that bothered me. A trap or a double cross was a foregone conclusion. No uncertainty there. It was a nagging feeling that I was underestimating the man called Zarpa. I was counting on using his impatient

greed as a lever. He was loner and I was assuming
the snatch was a solo operation. But what if I was
calling it wrong? What if Zarpa had managed to
recruit confederates? True, there had been only one
voice on the phone, but there was no guarantee
there would be only one kidnapper waiting at the
exchange point. If anyone showed at all.

Maybe—and this made me slip a little lower in the
seat—the plan was to hijack me on the Overseas
Highway. Pull alongside where the lanes briefly widened crossing Sugarloaf Key. Or bag me at a stop-
light. Señor Zarpa, I couldn't help remembering,
made a specialty of rip-offs.

The headlights following began to feel like twin
laser beams. Once, as a sedan pulled out to pass me,
I jammed on the brakes. The arms waving from the
open windows were attached to shrieking teenagers.
Joyriders. The rush of adrenaline woke up the pain
in my ankle and I began to regret not shooting the
dog. That raised a host of doubts. Would I be willing
to plug a two-legged beast, if it came to that?

I concentrated on what had been done to the little
girl and the palpable fear in Graham's voice.

"It's me, Daddy. I really fucked up."

Yes, indeed, and in a big way. So had Mommy
dearest. Was it toot that put the white fog of greed
in her brain and made her risk a seventeen-year-old
son against a swamp killer like Zarpa? Or had she
been fooled by the stories, always circulating in the
keys, about easy fortunes made in a single night?
The new, twisted version of the American Dream?

I didn't have any ready answers. All I had was a
suitcase of funny money and a .38 taped to my good
ankle and a willingness to trust to dumb luck. As for
Regina Chilly, whatever happened, she was a loser.
The look in her husband's eye was unmistakable. He
was willing to shrug off bankruptcy, but the risk to

the stepson he loved was not to be forgiven. After tonight, Reggie would be waltzing without him.

I crossed Saddlebunch without incident, driving east, the night air rushing in over the long hood of the coupe. On the Gulf side, Florida Bay was glassy calm, a mirror to the stars. On the Atlantic side the sea was furrowed, breaking hard against the low shore. I had the feeling, as I often did driving the Overseas Highway, that the tide had been out for centuries, that it was poised to rush back in at any moment, swallowing the string of keys in a single gulp.

At Cudjoe Key things began to unravel. I missed the turnoff for Cay Point and had to double back at Kemp Channel. The headlights were no longer in the rearview. Either they had turned first, or I was imagining things. I very much preferred the latter conclusion.

Cay Point Road was as I had remembered it. A mile or so of decaying pavement, put in over fill for an airport never built. Swamps of the ubiquitous mangrove to either side. I was beginning to develop a distrust for the hearty, water-rooted mangrove and the desolate, soggy landscape it formed. The search for Graham Chilly kept drawing me to shallow swamps and I did not trust swamps or the things that dwelled in them.

The road ended in a half-acre of paved parking lot. Over the years the heat had split the backtop. Low bushes had taken root in the fissures and the leaves brushed softly against the Caddy's undercarriage. I shut off the engine and listened to the night birds and the mangrove leaves rustling in the wind.

I got out, fighting the impulse to duck down. The moon was about half-full, with thin clouds scudding past. I got the suitcase out of the trunk and trudged toward the point, hiding the limp as best I could.

The path was overgrown, but not impossibly so. The flats around Cay Point were bonefish country in the late spring, and every year some intrepid, shore-based fisherman would take the trouble to cut back the growth.

By the time I got to the shore clearing, a point of ice seemed to have formed between my shoulder blades. The mangroves moved with the warm wind, hissing and creaking. My blood sparkled with adrenaline. I looked, in the mass of surrounding leaves, for the moon glint of a machete.

There is no beach at Cay Point, only a slab of compressed limestone that totals about a quarter acre. The rest of the area, maybe another three or four acres, is a thicket of red mangroves that are slowly pulling the shallow bottom up from the bay. I put the suitcase on the slab of rock, as instructed, and backed slowly away, almost convinced that I was the only human on the point.

I was listening so hard that the smell made no particular impression. I wasn't focused on smells. Quite the contrary. I was subconciously aware of rotting fish, the festering shells of stone crabs dropped by gulls, and the heavy, salt-drenched scent of the bay. I don't think I picked up on the pungent fumes of gasoline until I heard someone moving on the other side of the clearing, and even then I didn't know where the fumes were coming from. They seemed to be all around me.

Twigs snapped. Someone coughed. I dropped into a crouch and tried to focus in on the sound.

Two things happened in quick succession. A figure appeared in the path that led back to the parking lot. He was holding a cigarette or a lit match. I was reaching for the .38 when the mangroves exploded. A wall of air rushed in, followed instantly by a rising sheet of flames. I was belly down by then, arms over my head. There was another rush of air as more of the fumes ignited.

It took maybe twenty seconds for all of the spilled fuel to ignite. By then both the figure in the path and the suitcase full of loot was gone, from what I could see through the rolling smoke. The heat radiated rapidly. I backed into the water, keeping low, and was knee-deep before I remembered that the .38 was still taped to my ankle. By then the whole clearing area was afire.

Outflanked, outmaneuvered, and just plain outsmarted. A wave of nausea racked me, accompanied by the conviction that Graham Chilly was as good as dead. I dropped into the cool, shallow water and backstroked along the shore, trying to keep the splashing to a minimum. The fire raged on, spewing up roiling clouds of acrid smoke.

I flailed around in the waist-deep water for nearly thirty minutes before finding a clearing where I could get back ashore. By then I was so cold and miserable and mosquito-ravaged I didn't care if Zarpa was waiting to ambush me. As I dragged myself through the thick underbrush, the ankle throbbed with such force it seemed to glow in the dark.

Working toward the open area of the parking lot, where I could see the old coupe squatting like a faithful pooch. I tried to come up with a good explanation for Floyd Chilly, one that contained an element of hope.

I failed.

16

NO one in the Boca Chica Bar was the least disturbed by my swamp-slimed appearance, or my bleeding ankle, or the request for a dry cloth to clean the seawater from my gun. They were more interested in watching the exotic dancers or finding the bottoms of their glasses. Shrimpers, mostly, with a handful of gentlemen tourists out on a spree. Your typical hour-of-the-wolf crowd, with whiskey-glazed leers and specific desires. Dave Starky was there, defending his corner stool against all challengers. He asked, with mild curiosity, if I'd been wrassling gators again.

"I thought you were in Marathon," I said, "where they know how to move waterfront condos."

"Still waiting for the check to clear. Hey, you got your ammo all wet."

I sighted the inside of the empty barrel while the bartender watched impassively.

"You definitely need a drink, bubba," Dave said. "There's steam coming out of both ears."

I definitely did need a drink, but the definite drink did nothing to fill the emptiness, nor did it make the call to Floyd Chilly any easier. My report was short and in a sense pointless. I didn't know if Graham was alive or dead, or what Zarpa would do next.

"He didn't have the boy with him?" Floyd said, choosing his words carefully. The stereo was on in the background, loud and brassy.

"No."

"What do we do now?"

"We go to the police."

"That means it's too late," Floyd said. "Don't it?"

I told him I didn't know. That was the truth, strictly speaking. I had a cup of bar coffee as potent as blasting jelly and watched Dave Starky throw dollar bills at a Cuban stripper with sandshark eyes and unreal breasts. Dave explained, without my asking, that they were silicone, finest kind.

"Squeeze 'em and you know what happens?" He grinned. "They honk, like rubber duckies. I'm in love, bubba. This is the real thing."

They found Graham's Camaro in the Winn-Dixie parking lot. They being the Key West police, who had been called to the scene at three in the morning following reports of a Latin male attacking a parked sedan with a machete. The Latin male was nowhere to be found when the cops arrived.

"We have a beserk Cuban, a recovered missing vehicle that has been hacked up, and the shredded remains of several counterfeit fifties," Lieutenant Nelson Kerry said. "Naturally I think of you."

He handed me a Styrofoam container. I opened it and ate scrambled eggs, sausage, and biscuits without appetite while Nelly buttered his toast. We were in his office. Dawn was a slash of orange light through the window blinds. The coffee was hot, but I could not bring myself to drink it.

"What he must have done," I said, "he must have rolled a drum of aviation fuel out there before he made the call, then rigged a way to spill it over. I found two other drums out by the unfinished airstrip, both full. Stuff must be ten years old, but believe me it's still volatile."

"I can smell it on you," Kerry said, crunching the toast. "The smoke. Burned itself out, by the way. I guess you were so busy you forgot to call the fire department."

"I hate mangroves."

"From the look of it," he said, "they're not too fond of you, either. I suppose you don't know anything about the funny fifties?"

"Sure," I said. "They had Grant's picture on 'em."

"Had a rash of the same batch show up at the dog track last year. The T boys would love to talk with you, I'm sure."

"You called the Treasury Department?"

"We'll have to file a report, eventually."

I thought about Zach Malone and the pit bull that had tried to chew my ankle off, and I told Nelly about the money, leaving out names to protect the guilty.

"My, my," he said. "We been having a bad week, aint't we?"

"Not as bad as Graham Chilly is having."

"Uh huh," he said. "Well, my guess is his troubles are over."

Kerry reached into the paper bag on his desk and took out another Styrofoam container. This one was hamburger-sized. He snapped open the lid and showed me what was inside.

"We found it in the glove compartment of the Camaro," he said.

In the container was bloody fifty-dollar bill, folded in half. Nestled inside the fifty was a human ear. There was a thin hoop earring in the lobe.

Kerry said, "I guess Zarpa is pretty pissed off about the money, huh?"

There was a green lizard on the screen, watching

me with tiny black eyes. Dark diamond points and a flickering tongue.

From the hammock I said, "Don't stick that thing out at me, buster."

The lizard skittered to the top of the screen and froze, blending into the green background of the ficus tree. I felt safe in the hammock, suspended above the hard meanness of the earth.

I'd been out to Palmetto Key again and it hadn't been a pretty visit. Floyd had taken it very badly. He was convinced, as Nelson Kerry was, that the boy was dead. He didn't say it was my fault because he didn't need to put it in words. As for Regina, she decided the severed ear couldn't possibly belong to her son.

"Okay, Graham wore one of those silly little hoops, but so what? There are thousands of men who wear earrings in Key West," she announced, using a logic reinforced with whatever it was she was taking to stave off reality. "And anyhow, you don't die from having your ear removed. There's a man down on Duval Street who's missing *both* ears, and he's still fresh enough to pinch every girl that walks by."

She was wearing dark sunglasses that veiled her eyes, a palm-green cotton blazer with the resort logo on the breast, and matching pleated skirt. Dressed for success. Carlos was loading her bags in the trunk of her leased BMW. I hadn't noticed the vanity plates before: FAMOUS. Reggie would be staying at the resort, she informed me, "for the time being."

"When Graham comes home we'll just reassess the situation," she said, holding tight to her purse with both hands, "that's what we'll do."

I lay in the hammock, reassessing my own situation. With the police informed and the FBI notified of the abduction, there was no room for an unlicensed search-and-rescue operative. And it now seemed obvious that the authorities should have been part of the game plan from the beginning. The severed ear made Graham's complicity in a drug scheme irrelevant.

As for the ear, the forensic lab had already determined the blood type, useful only in that it did not eliminate Graham as the victim. As a tissue sample it was now evidence, conceivably, of a homicide. Further tests would determine if it had been removed from a living body. Morbid speculation around the station house was that it might well be the only evidence, since the psychological profile of Zarpa suggested he was capable of finding effective and imaginative ways to make a body disappear.

"After seeing what he did to that Camaro," Kerry said, "I figure the guy is a human Cuisinart. Makes the sushi chef at the Half Shell look like an amateur."

Cops will have their dark little jokes. The pathologist, a former emergency-room sawbones from Elizabeth, New Jersey, was worse. "Think of it not as an ordinary human ear," he'd said to me. "Think of it as a slice of life."

Think of it, Stash, as the flesh of a terrified boy. Lie there in your string hammock, on your screened-in porch, trading insults with a mute lizard as the palm fronds rattle against the tin roof. Think of it as a field study in failure. Think of it as a bad call, the breaks, the way the cookie crumbles. Think of it and keep on thinking; the thinking is penance.

Meanwhile, back at the mangrove swamp, Zarpa the Claw is doing something small and awful with a sharp machete.

When it becomes necessary to ease the mind, or seek communion, or find inner peace—however you care to describe the condition—I go out on the water. An imaginary sign hangs somewhere in the frontal lobes: GONE FISHING.

Mutt was beside himself. He followed me from the bait shack to the dock and appeared ready to leap into the boat to finish the argument.

"This boggles the brain," he said, rubbing the furrowed brown baldness of his head. "This beats all. I got three different parties just dyin' to hook permit, and the laziest guide in Key West wants to go fishin' *alone*."

"Book 'em with Tom Skelton. He's the permit genius in these parts."

"Grrrr," Mutt growled, scuffing his bare feet on the dock. "I knew you'd say that. Just so happens Skelton's full up and you've been known to find a few permit yourself. Hell, it's a bonefish tide, comes to that. They'd settle for bonefish. Stash, honey, they'd settle for mangrove snapper, if you put the charm on."

"Don't say that word."

"Huh?"

"Mangrove. *Verboten*, Now, have you got some live mullet in that well or do I have to net some myself?"

Mutt did his war dance, circling tight around a piling, his eyes bugging out. "Tarpon," he shouted. "The boy wants to hook a tarpon! Any damn fool can hook on to a tarpon, you don't need to leave this *dock* to hook a tarpon."

I asked him how much of a cut he was expecting if he succeeded in booking me out with the permit fanciers. He almost swallowed his cigar.

"Well, don't that just fry it. A fellah tries to help out a young man fancies himself a fishing guide, and he gets money throwed in his face."

He stomped off to his shack and returned with a white plastic bucket.

"Here's your damn mullet," he said.

I poured the baitfish into the well at the stern. "I'll make it up to you, Mutt. Give me a couple of days, okay? Book me a party next week. Tide won't really be right for permit until then anyhow."

He sighed, scratching at the hard disk of his belly. "Just keep that bad ankle out of the water," he advised, "or a shark'll have you for lunch."

The wind, what there was of it, was out of the northeast. I headed for the flats near Pelican Key, which would be in the lee if the breeze held. After clearing Whitehead Spit I put her on a plane, kicking spray that was intended to wet the gawkers at the Casa Marina pier. From there I cut outside, leaving Smathers Beach astern, unable to quite erase the image of Trudy and her brand-new romance with Duane from Nebraska.

At Pelican I cut the outboard and drifted in over a sandy bottom, tufted here and there with beards of turtle grass. If I'd been after permit or bonefish, truly shallow fish, I'd have poled into knee-deep water. But I wanted to dance with a tarpon, and a dancing-size fish needs about four feet of water when it rolls to gulp for air. I wasn't going to fool around trying the purist routine with light tackle and hand-tied flies, either. I didn't have the patience that day, and neither would old *megalops*, not in the heat of the afternoon.

The mullet Mutt had provided were small and lively. Likely to tempt a human-sized tarpon even if it wasn't particularly hungry. As *Bushwhacked* drifted on the incoming tide, I rigged up a heavy wire leader and a number-five hook and slipped it into a mullet. I left it there in the well, where it circled cleanly, as if the impaled hook didn't bother it in the slightest. Then I moved to the bow and began to study the flats.

Looking down through water so clear it seemed but an illusion, I saw a school of small, yellowtail snapper hovering over the bottom, facing the incoming tide. A patch of turtle grass was home to a myriad of tiny silverfish. A big ray, wider than *Bushwhacked*, drifted by like a spotted cloud, tail switching. I lay there with my chin in my hands, content to drift all afternoon, maybe forever. Then, thirty yards to the left, a tarpon squawked at me.

The tarpon, as the textbooks will tell you, has a primitive kind of lung and comes to the surface regularly to replenish air. It liked to roll with a sudden crack of its tail, as if biting chunks of oxygen from the sky. At night you can hear the peculiar, gasping noise it makes, a kind of fishy wheeze. That's when it prefers to feed, after the sun goes down and its bulk is not so visible, but instinct will make it strike a mullet, if the mullet looks sweet.

"Are you sweet?" I whispered to the trembling baitfish, lifting it from the well. "Are you irresistible?"

I stripped line from the reel, placed the mullet over the side, and patted its bottom. Off you go, darling. Lunchtime.

The mullet proved irresistible in the sense that it wanted to swim anywhere but in range of the tarpon, who circled the shallows lazily. There was only so much coaxing I could do with the line, leading the persnickety little mullet. Casting the thing would have risked stunning it, so I just kept hoping that the mullet's path would cross with the roving tarpon before the hook killed it.

Meanwhile I watched the tarpon and the tarpon watched me, or more probably *Bushwhacked*. Once or twice it changed course with a flick of its tail and nosed over toward the baitfish. Just as abruptly it would depart, roll to the surface, and bite the air. As if to say, Kiss my ass, human.

This went on for a while. I got lazy, waiting, and lost sight of the big fish as it passed under the boat. It must have altered course in *Bushwhacked*'s shadow, because it hit the mullet on a run before I was set to react. The slack line was snapped up instantly. It was only instinct that made me pull back on the tip of the rod, setting the hook.

I had wanted a dance. The tarpon, as if bored with the feinting game, obliged, exploding from the water fifty feet away. It writhed violently as it tried to loose the hook from its great jutting underjaw. It reentered with a noisy, shuddering splash. I was ready when, a few heartbeats later, it stood up and began to tail-dance backward, taking yards of line with each flick of its powerful fins. A hundred pounds, easy.

As it slipped beneath the surface, the fish looked surprised at not having shed the hook or severed the leader. Probably it had been hooked before with light tackle and spit back the fly or lure after a couple of head shakes. But the number-five held to the bony jaw, setting deeper with each run.

I wanted to feel the weight of the fish, the heart and muscle of the fight inside it. I wanted to feel exhausted, spent, emptied of thought. I wanted to feel each ritualized twitch of the tail-dance transmitted by the singing nerve of filament line. I wanted to be hypnotized by sunlight glistening off prehistoric scales. I wanted, most of all, to forget.

After forty minutes my arms were vulcanized. I was tempted to set an anchor, so the big fish couldn't drag me offshore, but couldn't risk fouling. Every now and then the tarpon would collapse and lie in the shallows, gasping noisily. Reeling in was a problem without crew to pole *Bushwhacked*, because at the least tension in the line the tarp would fling himself up again, like a middleweight rising suddenly from the canvas, glassy-eyed and dangerous.

And so we danced, two punch-drunks on an ebbing tide. A row of stump-seated cormorants was our impassive audience, black-winged and silent as they ranged along the shore. When the tarpon finally lay exhausted in the shallows, I lolled in the bottom of *Bushwhacked*, utterly depleted. Empty and satisfied. An osprey circled overhead, alerted to the matinee performance, regretting, perhaps, that both performers were of a size too large to take.

When I had regained enough strength to make my adrenaline-parched limbs behave, I set the anchor and slipped over the side into the cool, waist-deep water. The tarpon watched me approach. The long trailing dorsal fin had picked up a strand of turtle grass. It looked, in the light, like a glistening emerald necklace.

The big fish trembled as I ran my hand over the hard, armorlike scales. The hook was protruding through the bone of the underslung jaw. You could see where it had almost straightened out. Another round or two and the tarpon would have been free. I cut the heavy wire leader off with a pair of pliers and snipped off the hook barb. The rest would be up to the fish. As spent and toothless as it appeared, I was unwilling to put my fingers in its mouth. Too many tales of supposedly comatose tarpon nipping digits neatly off for a nightmare knuckle sandwich.

As sometimes happens, the fish was too weak from the fight to move. I steered it upright and began to walk, forcing water through the gills. The tarpon was as docile as a fairground pony. This was endgame dance, the last slow waltz. Along the shore the cormorants applauded, raising oily wings.

After a few turns the tarpon began to swim on its

own. Slowly, and with immense dignity, its great tail came to life. I released it and backed away.

"Have a nice day," I called out as it circled away. The cormorants, who appreciate irony, laughed like drunken geese.

When I got back to Mutt's dock the sun was touching down and Lily Cashman was waiting with bad news.

17

WE repaired to the Laughing Gull, where Lily and Sam ordered sundowners, the kind with three species of rum. I was still suffering the effects of too much alcohol over too many days and opted for iced tea.

"I just got the paperwork today," Lily said. "It was drawn up six weeks ago, to take effect afer thirty days."

"Which means it was in effect just before Graham disappeared?"

She nodded.

"Does Floyd know there's a two-million-dollar policy on the boy?"

"I don't know. From the look of it, Reggie is the one who filled out the forms. Graham is her son, after all. Floyd will have to know, sooner or later, because the term payment came out of the condo cash flow. I wanted to talk to you first. I heard he was in bad shape."

The basin was virtually empty of boats. There was clear weather in the Gulf and the shrimp were running. At the wharf a fat Cuban woman and three skinny girls were repairing a black seine net. In the crepuscular light they looked like Lilliputians fabricating a giant net stocking. This was reasonable enough, in a world upside down.

"This is unbelievable," I said. "Less than twenty-four hours ago Reggie was trying to convince me

Graham had to be alive and well. Now you're telling me she's trying to collect on a two-million-dollar policy on his life?"

"A million even," Lilly responded. "Double indemnity for accidental death. Murder, according to the actuaries, is an accident."

"But they haven't found a body."

"Not all of it."

Sam said, "Gross," and sipped her bloodred cocktail.

"What Reggie wants to do, she tells me, is get the paperwork started," Lilly explained. "She had identified the body part as belonging to Graham. I have a deposition from the coroner to that effect."

"She *what*?"

"Reggie says it's the kid's earring. American Life Equity will hold up the payment process as long as it can because that's the nature of insurance companies, but the Chillys have a case, even if the body is never recovered." Lilly smiled grimly and ticked off the reasons on salmon-pink fingernails. "They filed a missing-child report, they hired an investigator— that's you—and they have a tape recording of a death threat. Every aspect of the situation is consistent with an abduction and murder."

"This is so gross," Sam said, "I can hardly believe I'm hungry. Anybody for crab claws?"

It had been a long day. I felt old and brittle, unable to absorb this new information. There was a realistic bias to my understanding of human nature and its capacity to astound and betray, but I could not find a place in the scheme of things for a mother with a heart so cold. It was one thing for Regina Chilly to blind herself to the risk her son was taking; it was another thing entirely to gamble on odds that he would not return alive.

"I asked her about the timing," Lilly said. "She

claims it was pure coincidence. A normal precaution in a family-owned business."

"Let me get this straight. The Palmetto Key Time-Share Resort is on the verge of bankruptcy and she decides to pay twenty-five grand for a term-insurance policy on the life of her son? That's a normal precaution?"

"Not exactly," Lily said as Sam returned with a basket of cold crab claws. "It was a three-way policy, originally. Twelve-month term on the three of them, Reggie, Floyd, and the boy. American Life Equity refused to cover Floyd because of his history of alcohol abuse."

Sam slurped her drink through the single white fang of a straw and pushed the basket of claws my way. I declined. Kurt Hansen sauntered out to the wharf, accompanied by two gentlemen in tropical-weight business suits. Government paper-pushers, not field agents. Hansen was showing them the sights, strutting his stuff among the natives. His toothy grin iced up when he spotted me at the tiki bar.

"Heard about your, ah, misfortune," he said, ignoring Lily and Sam. "That's the way it goes sometimes."

"Yep," I agreed. "That's the way. Anything new on Señor Zarpa? He blipped on your screens?"

"Not a clue. Probably hightailed it to Tampa. Maybe Miami."

"Right," I said. "Maybe Miami."

Hansen sat down with the suits and said something. The suits laughed and made a point of not looking at me. I made a point of not getting up and throwing Kurt Hansen in the basin. Maybe Miami indeed—said in such a way there was no doubt he knew a lot more than maybe Miami.

"Who's the dweeb with all the gold chain?" Sam wanted to know.

"A big wheel," I said. "Count the spokes if you don't believe me."

"T.D. is in one of his moods," Lily said. "He's had a bad week."

I'd been beat up, bitten, and blown up. I'd been shat on by a bird called Lautrec and winked at by a guy named Duane. I'd been set up and lied to and left for dead. I'd had bad dreams and bugs in my teeth and my best girl was going back to Nebraska. All things considered, it had been a bad week. Indeed it had.

"See how he's grinding his teeth?" Sam giggled. "Looks mean enough to bite rocks."

"T.D. has that easygoing conch attitude," Lily observed. "But Gawd a'mighty, this boy *hates* to lose."

"So who's this Zarpa person that's got our boy so bent out of shape?" Sammie said, licking Dijon sauce from her lips. "I say we go find him and bust his ass."

I explained, wearily, that people who went to find Zarpa had a tendency to disappear. Sam curled her wrist, flexed an impressive bicep, and said, Show me the son of a bitch. Then she blew on her nails to show how she would dust him. I happened to mention that if Zarpa couldn't best her in hand-to-hand combat, he certainly had her beat in the fingernail department.

"He's got these long talons," I said. "Like a mandarin. You ask me, there's something kinky about having nails that long."

Sammie had a funny look in her dark eyes.

"A Cuban with fingernails like that hangs around the beach," she said thoughtfully. "Down by where the hawkers set up? Real strange dude."

I asked her what she meant by strange.

"Dunno," she said, shaking her head. Her glossy black bangs shimmered. "The kind of strange that makes your skin crawl. One time he comes over and he tells me he wants to rent a canoe. This heavy accent, I could hardly understand, but that's what he had the hots for, a canoe. I try to explain how I only rent windsurfers, but he wouldn't take no for an answer. Man, you should have seen the look in his eye. Like he was going to eat me alive."

"Zarpa," I said. "Had to be Zarpa."

"I couldn't shake the guy. He was like getting very agitated, you know? I was about ready to call the cops when Paula came over and calmed him down."

A small, clear bell went off in my head.

"Paula?"

"Yeah, a cute little number," Sam said. "Sells her watercolors along the wall at the beach, or sometimes you'll see her at Mallory Dock. Really nice pictures. Lots of greens and pinks. This weenie with the long fingernails, he used to hang around her, like."

"Paula have a last name?"

"I suppose she does, but I don't know it. Just Paula the painter. Lives in a houseboat, somebody told me, over Coral Canal way."

The bell became chimes, then lights, camera, action. I threw some money on the table and gave Sam a big wet kiss. Then I started to jog along the waterfront, the blood pounding in my ears.

18

MUTT was sitting on a trap, his cigar glowing like an afterburner.

" 'Course I refueled your boat," he said. "Ain't got nothing better to do than wait hand and foot on the laziest, most contrary conch in Key West."

Unhitching the stern line, I asked about the latest update on the offshore weather.

"A foot of chop in the bay. Ocean side is glassy," he said, rising from the trap to man the bow line. "Don't tell me you still got tarpon fever?"

"Zarpa fever," I said. "I'm going to see a girl about a guy."

I put it in gear, cleared the dock, and made the tight turn into the basin. Mutt followed out to the end of the wharf, drawing hot red squiggles in the air as he gestured with his cigar, "Keep your head down," he shouted after me. "Don't take no wooden nickles!"

Sometimes at night, on certain tides, a boat cuts a wake that opens in the darkness and glows. They say the luminous trail is caused by a kind of phosphorescent plankton. All I know for sure is that the eerie beauty of it will mesmerize anyone who stares too long. I am convinced that some of Key West's famous wrecks were caused not by storm or reef, but by helmsmen lost in the hypnotic dream of the glowing wake. Watching the stars spill up like fireflies through the furrow, they let their ships sail on, straight to destruction.

For some reason the phosphorescence made me think of Kurt Hansen and his airborne radar screens: the DEA mapping the glowworm trails of ships at sea, converging on small craft, and redhaired fishermen, and bales of southern weed.

Maybe Miami.

My ass, Miami. Zarpa was out there somewhere, in whatever swamp he'd chosen to hole up in. He still had Graham Chilly, dead or alive, and it was unlikely he'd given up on the prospect of separating Famous Floyd from his wealth. Kurt Hansen knew that much, I was convinced. He just didn't give a damn. Or maybe he wanted to see me get in so deep I would have to beg for help and agree to become one of his informants.

Fat chance. Before ratting for Hansen I'd cut sugarcane for Castro, or wait on table at Pier House, or drink lye—all prospects of equal attraction.

As for Regina Chilly and her morbid arrangment with American Life Equity, I didn't know what to think. Failing to make a major drug deal, had she and her son hatched up a bogus abduction scheme that had gone awry? If that was the case, why hadn't they gotten ransom insurance, rather than accidental death? Was Floyd in on it? Could the man with the gravelly baritone and the watery blue eyes and the hangdog face have fooled me so completely?

I looked to the curling wake for answers and found only this: a boy's voice, trembling with fear. Finding Graham. That's what I had promised to do. The rest of it didn't matter.

There were lights on at Coral Canal. The reflection of the barge, reversed in the still backwaters of the canal, was a dark blot punctuated by flickering yellow rectangles.

I could have cut the engine in the Stock Island channel and poled my way in. But I had nothing to hide. I was tired of stealth and intrigue and games of chance.

As I brought *Bushwhacked* alongside the houseboat, the details sharpened. I could see the interior of the cabin, the kerosene lamps illuminating it. I could see the figure crouched on the bow of the barge, in approximately the same place where the pelican had mocked me.

"Don't move," Paula Davis said. "I've got a gun."

I cut the engine. "Then go on and shoot," I said. "It's the only thing hasn't happened to me yet."

"Oh," she said, standing up. "The narc. Or are you a guide?"

"Just for tonight," I said, "try thinking of me as a friend of Graham Chilly."

There was just enough light spilling from the cabin so her chin and lips were visible. She smiled. "I thought you never met Graham," she said.

"I been carrying his picture around in my pocket. That makes him a friend."

What Paula had in her hands was not a gun, but a coiled line. She pulled in on it. On the end was a brace of small red snapper, looped through the gills.

"I'm about to have supper," she said. "Care to join me?"

Right away I noticed a couple of interesting things about Ms. Davis. She knew how to clean a snapper without wasting motion or fish, and there were pale freckles splashed over her prominent cheekbones. Also she had elegantly proportioned limbs, nice muscle tone, and dark-lashed brown eyes that, in the lamplight, looked flecked with gold. The effect was spoiled only slightly by a certain know-it-all pout that, as I discovered, was easily dissolved by a ready smile.

"Watch the noodle," she cautioned. "Max head-room is five-ten."

I was used to ducking through low cabins and kept down, moving from the galley sink to a seat at the dining table without straightening up. I gazed around at the neatly arranged interior of the house-boat, while Paula, wearing cutoff khaki shorts and a sleeveless blouse cinched over her bare navel, sea-soned and breaded the fillets, then pan-fried them in olive oil on a camp stove. The crisp smell did won-ders for my appetite. There was plenty of fresh Cu-ban bread frosted with butter and a side of black beans with a marinated onion garnish. I ate steadily until it was gone, then polished the empty plate with a heel of bread and grinned, high on carbo-hydrates.

"Funny," I said as Paula brewed strong, sweet-ened Bustelo coffee. "I had you figured more for the granola type."

"Because I'm an artist? Well, pardon me for going against stereotype, but we humans are omnivores, okay? It's bred in our teeth and our intestines. Why deny a million years of human evolution? So if it's fresh I'll eat it."

With a full belly and a hit of caffeine I was ready to pop the question. "I'm looking for Zarpa. You know, the carnivore? Used to hang out with you at Smathers Beach, I believe."

Paula gave me a long look. The know-it-all pout made her look vexing, but not unattractive. "I do know Zarpa," she said, "but I don't know where he is. He doesn't, as the saying goes, have a fixed abode."

"He's got Graham," I said. "He may have killed him already."

Rumor travels fast along the waterfront. Paula had already heard about the counterfeit money and the severed ear. The implication of murder was why she was willing to talk about Zarpa and Graham and how she inadvertently brought them together. I let her tell it slow, and in pieces, and kept the interruptions to a minimum.

"What I've been doing," she said, "I've been painting my way down the East Coast. Three years ago I was in New Hampshire, in the fine-arts program at the university. Studio painting, which means oils and acrylics. Emphasis on color value and brush technique and formal studies, okay? Take my word, it was a very academic approach, solid and plodding and entirely devoid of inspiration. It's the game you play if you want an advanced degree so that you can get a tenured position teaching other people how to get tenured positions. What happened, one day I got sick of the bullshit. Packed up my gear and went up to Bar Harbor, Maine, and got a job waitressing part-time so I could paint full-time. I loved it. I was doing good stuff. Fresh. Watercolors, mostly, on a tight format. Postcard size, right?"

"Like this stuff you've got thumbtacked to the bulkhead?" I said, looking at a dozen or so color sketches of the Coral Canal environs.

"Similar," she said. "Although you won't find that shade of green in Maine, not ever."

"I like them," I said. "I think they're very good."

"They're okay," she said without any particular emphasis. "I'm still learning."

"You were in Maine," I reminded her, "where the green is a different shade."

We were sitting opposite each other at the small galley table, drinking second coffees. Our knees tended to bump. I was aware of the mingled scents of coffee, sea air, and the clean, natural body perfume of a young woman. In all ways a highly attractive person. Graham's obsession with her was easily comprehended. A grown man might easily fall under her spell; an emotionally immature adolescent, dazzled by hormones, wouldn't stand a chance.

"From Bar Harbor I went south to Cape Cod. That's where I started selling stuff. Along the street in P-town or at the docks in Hyannis."

She continued south with the seasons, or sometimes with a man. There had been a scalloper in the Chesapeake and then, briefly, a sailor in Virginia Beach.

"It didn't work out, but he's the guy got me thinking about the keys. He'd been stationed down here and he went on and on about the reefs and the way light appears to shine up through the water. It made me think I'd like to paint the place. Just grab a handful of that light, you know?"

Our knees bumped again, gently, as the houseboat swung around into the wind. I liked the feeling and Paula didn't seem to mind.

"So that's how you happened to be living on a barge in Coral Canal."

"Well," she said, "there's more, but that's basically it. How I met Graham was at Mallory Dock. He bought one of my sketches. My first impression was he was about twelve years old. That baby face, you know?"

"It's there in the snapshot," I said, "that baby face."

"Next day he brought me flowers. Gardenias."

"A romantic kid," I said.

"That's Graham, okay. He had a practical way of attracting my attention, too, which was to buy up every piece of work I put out. It got embarrassing. Like I was teasing the kid with my art. It got so bad, finally, the only way he'd agree to leave me alone was if I'd do him."

My eyebrows went up. Paula laughed.

"You know," she said. "Paint his portrait."

That was how Graham, maddeningly persistent, had first managed to get himself aboard *Green Flash*. Paula removed a black portfolio, one of several, from a plywood shelf, and opened it on the galley table. Inside were quick charcoal sketches with heavy corrections laid over in dark pencil. The face in the charcoal smudges was unfocused, as if the subject couldn't sit still, which was, Paula said, the case.

"He kept coming around to my side, wanting to see what I was doing. How I thought he looked. Very excited about the whole process, okay? It was like trying to sketch a puppy dog."

Indeed, I thought, only it wasn't Graham's tail that had been wagging. "What did he talk about," I asked, "while you were doing him?"

She thought about it, staring into the coffeecup so the heavy lashes hid her eyes. "Mostly his father."

"His father or his stepfather?"

She looked up. "I didn't know there was a stepfather. It was always Dad this, Dad that. How successful his father was, what a great relationship they had, stuff like that. I figured, well, old Famous Floyd must have more to him than you'd guess after seeing those low-rent TV promotions."

"How about his mother?"

"Never said much, but I got the impression she spoiled him."

Paula put aside the charcoal sketches and brought out another portfolio. As she opened it the irritating pout spread over her lips again.

"You're wondering if I ever slept with him," she said. "I did. But only once, okay? And it was a bad idea, like I knew it would be. It happened after I started painting Zarpa."

Painting Zarpa. A harmless-enough phrase that in another context might suggest the premise of one of those sophisticated modern novels in which nothing much happens. Ennui-ridden yuppies donning designer-knit mantles of suburban angst, that sort of thing. But out there in the mangrove-encrusted canal the idea of painting Zarpa made a chill flick down my spine. A cold, spectral finger of dread, fresh from the swamp.

Some of the Zarpa watercolors had almost a snapshot clarity. As in the sketches of Graham, the face was always indistinct, but the body, especially the hands with the long, curving fingernails, was rendered in detail. In one of the pictures, which reminded me of something by Thomas Eakins, Zarpa posed in a canoe, holding the paddle horizontal to his naked torso. The canal behind him was blurred with mist. The shoulder-length black hair emphasized his Indio blood. He looked like a primitive warrior, as deadly and sudden as a squall.

"That was my first," Paula said, touching another sketch, her finger blotting out his face. "Down at Mallory Dock it's too crowded to work, so I just sell stuff I've already done. But at the beach sometimes I paint right there, because it attracts an audience. Good for business. One afternoon I noticed Zarpa sitting just like that on the top of the wall. That moody, mysterious Indian look, and the bizarre fingernails, you couldn't help but notice. I start to do him. Then I look up and he's disappeared. He comes back, never says a word, I start doing him again. Blink, he's gone. Finally I said I'd pay him to sit still, and that's how he started modeling for me."

"You paid him?"

"Sure. By then Graham had started to buy up my stuff and I had a little extra. So I paid Zarpa. He really loved that, getting money from a woman."

Just one of the things Zarpa loved. Another was inflicting pain. "Graham was jealous at first. He assumed I was sleeping with Zarpa, because I did some nude studies of him. But doing Zarpa was like getting a rattlesnake to pose, okay? He was pretty and kind of handsome in a dangerous way, but you wouldn't want him in your bed. Not that he ever came on to me. I never got the idea he wanted sex, not in the normal way . . ." She let it drift.

I thought of the kind of things a man like Zarpa wanted, and the cold finger tickled my spine again.

"Anyhow, Graham was going nuts about how he just had to prove his love to me and one day he kept after me for so long I just gave up and took him to bed."

"And for Graham that was declaration of undying love?"

"You got it. It was right after that he started talking about how he was going to make a big score and save the resort for his mom and dad. I thought it was just hot air."

"It was," I said. "Only Graham didn't know it."

Paula got up from the galley table, breaking the intimacy of knee-to-knee contact.

"You really think he killed Graham?" she asked, staring out at the dark, still waters of the canal.

"I won't know that," I said, "until I find Zarpa."

Something in the barge moved.

"Did you feel that?"

Paula shook her head, puzzled.

"Like the weight just shifted," I said.

I moved to the screen door and squinted. There was an empty canoe floating next to where I'd tied *Bushwhacked* to the barge.

"Get down," I said.

I was bending down to get the .38 from where it was taped to my ankle when two bare feet exploded through the screen and caught me full in the face.

The next thing I was aware of was being flat on

my back with the taste of blood in my mouth. The two bare and filthy feet were planted firmly on my chest. They were attached to the man called Zarpa, who crouched over me, holding a machete to my throat.

"Ho ho," he said thickly. "You look for Zarpa. Zarpa look for you. Is very funny, yes?"

"Yes," I said, making an effort to sound agreeable.

Keeping the edge of the blade firm against the softest part of my neck, he reached with his free hand and confiscated the gun. He looked at it and beamed. Merry Christmas and happy birthday, too. He aimed the .38 at Paula, who was hefting a black iron fry pan.

"*Ponlo pa, abajo*," he said.

She knelt and put the frying pan on the deck.

"Hokay," he said, moving off of me. "*Levántate.*"

I stood up. The end of the machete was sharpened to a point. He demonstrated that by putting it in the center of my chest and pushing. I backed away until the bulkhead made it impossible to retreat any further.

"*Voltéate.*"

"What?" I said, playing dumb.

The blade pricked through the thin layer of skin over my breastbone. I could feel the blood running down inside my shirt.

"*Voltéate*," Zarpa grunted. "*Rápido.*"

I turned around. Out of the corner of my eye I could see the machete flashing in the lamp light as he raised it over my head. The blade came down and the lights, as the saying goes, went out. I fell into a black funnel as the world spun into darkness.

19

I woke up in the bottom of my own guide boat, expertly trussed with a length of half-inch anchor line and gagged with a foul-tasting rag. The back of my head was caked with clotted blood, from where Zarpa had crowned me with the flat of the blade. Paula was next to me, facedown and similarly bound. There were stars overhead and a dark figure at the helm. He had the 140-horse outboard wide open. I could feel in my ribs the way the hull was slamming into the chop.

I remembered Mutt saying he'd topped off the fuel tanks. Full up, *Bushwhacked* had range throughout Florida Bay, or to Cuba, for that matter, which was interesting to contemplate.

In between hull slams I writhed, trying to work the bonds loose. I got nowhere, but Zarpa decided to discourage any further effort by hitting my bare forearms with the flat of the machete, breaking open the skin. This was very discouraging indeed. I stopped writhing and lay as still as it was possible to lie in a heaving boat.

I was in a pretty good mood, considering. My head was still attached to my shoulders, and that was important to me. Paula was concious, as evidenced by the gasping noise she made as the hull hammered the swells. If we were alive, maybe Graham Chilly was still hanging in there.

After a while I was able to orient myself to the stars. The Pleiades, the Cross, the bright familiars of the southern sky told me Zarpa was headed northeast. The frequency of the chop made me think we were in the bay. Out on the Atlantic side the swell would have been deeper, had more roll. The bay made sense because there were hundreds of small uninhabited keys within a few miles of shore. Mangrove keys, mostly, and our abductor had a proven affinity for mangroves.

It is difficult to gauge time when you are trussed like a chicken in the bottom of a careening guide boat. I was more concerned with distance run than time, so I tried counting swells. Got to four hundred and something when he changed direction, slamming me hard into Paula's side. I could hear her groan even over the high-pitched whine of the outboard. From the shift in the Southern Cross it appeared he had veered north about five points. I started counting swells again. It was tricky because *Bushwhacked* was taking them at a different angle and the banging was not so regular. I had a count of two hundred and six when he lowered the throttle. *Bushwhacked* came off her plane and began to wallow.

You could feel it, the difference in the water. We were out of the channel and into the shallows. Zarpa stood up at the wheel. He steered with one hand as he peered through the darkness. Sighting a landmark or a buoy, I assumed. There was a very familiar-looking pistol jammed in the pocket of his frayed jeans. Nelson Kerry would not be pleased with how easily I'd let it get into a felon's possession. The machete was wedged between the console and the rear seat, way out of my range even if my hands had been free.

Bushwhacked came to an abrupt stop. I kept going, sliding along the bottom until the top of my head bumped into the forward seat locker, stunning me. The next thing I knew I was facedown in cool, shallow water. I coughed. Fingers laced themselves into my hair and jerked my face out of the water. Then I was stumbling as Zarpa took hold of the ropes and hauled me ashore. A flock of birds exploded from the mangrove branches as he pushed me forward. Before the stiff leaves blinded me I caught a glimpse of *Bushwhacked* with her bow jammed up against the thick mangrove roots. Inside the boat Paula was curled into a fetal position, motionless.

My captor had a marvelous knowledge of knots and how to tie them. A nice neat sheepshank held my ankles about ten inches apart, just enough to let me shuffle along the path, encouraged by the fist that kept thumping me in the small of the back, and by proximity of the machete blade. The same machete, I supposed, had cut the trail through the dense undergrowth. A thin, damp slot through the wilderness, as black as midnight fog.

The chopped branch ends tore at me like cat claws. Blinded by blood and sweat and tears, I was aware of the clearing more by the lack of scratching than by visual confirmation. I heard Zarpa panting, felt his breath hot on the back of my neck. Then he pushed and I fell heavily to the ground. I rolled over on my back and worked at blinking my eyes clear.

A flare of light pierced the darkness. The flare became a glow as Zarpa adjusted a Coleman lantern. Gradually my vision adjusted and I could make out the shadowy boundaries of the clearing. A rough circle maybe fifteen yards in circumference. Where Zarpa had hung the lantern was the crumbling remains of a fishing shanty. A camp, I assumed, long since abandoned. The tin on the shed roof was rusted through in a thousand places and the poles that held it up had sagged. Mere inertia kept it from total collapse. That and mangrove branches entwined through the rotted framework.

A new tarp had been rigged over a portion of the shed. Under it, glittering in the lantern light, were the shiny new things Zarpa had brought to his nest: three or four fuel cans, a camp stove, a five-gallon water cooler, several canteens, an assortment of aluminum pots and cups. Old Zarpa was a regular Boy Scout, what with the camping gear and his expertise in knot tying. I wondered how many trips he'd had to make in the canoe, transporting the stuff out to this desolate, sea-level jungle.

The lantern floated toward me. Zarpa placed it a foot or so from my face. His fingernails were thick and yellowed, like ivory, and were the only clean thing about him. Crouching, he exuded a swampy pong, a powerful, eye-watering whiff of decay. His eyes were black and glassy. Alligator eyes.

"How you?" he said, cutting loose the gag. "You okay now?"

The voice he used was as cool and sweet as sugar venom. He laid the flat of the machete blade against my cheek and stroked. A butcher testing the suppleness of his meat.

"Hokay?"

The blade pressed harder until I nodded. Okay is a relative term. I was not dead, therefore I was okay.

"*Bueno*," he whispered. "*Hoy día, gran regalo, comprendes?*"

He rose from the crouch and moved toward the shack while I waited for Zarpa's "big surprise." A number of grisly scenarios flashed on the screen of my mind. Charnel-house scenes. I renewed the struggle with the bonds as I watched him rummage through the shack. All I succeeded in doing was cutting off the circulation to my hands.

Zarpa returned with an oblong shape under his

arm. He crouched again, placing the plastic box near my face. It took a moment for me to bring it into focus. A portable radio/cassette player, popularly known as a boom box or ghetto blaster. He pressed one of the shiny plastic buttons. Cuban salsa music stunned my ears. Radio Martí, from the sound of it. After another button was pushed and the sound ceased as abruptly as it had begun.

Zarpa patted the portable cassette player. "She is Sony," he said. *"Un buen sonido, muy alto."*

Yes, indeed, it was good and loud. Loud enough to make me ring like a trussed-up tuning fork when he pressed the button to demonstrate. At elevated decibels, Radio Martí feels like an ice pick piercing your eardrum. To make sure I got the full effect, my new pal Zarpa held my head against the speaker.

As an instrument of Oriental torment, your Sony blaster is more effective than water torture. My head felt like the gong the Moocher kicked around in the Cab Calloway song.

"Hokay," Zarpa said when he judged me sufficiently tenderized. *"Más tarde* we talk, you talk, *comprendes?"*

I didn't *comprendes* anything but the pain and the clammy sweat of fear. I was afraid of Zarpa as I had never been afraid of anything except, possibly, the kind of large poisonous snake that occurs only in nightmares. Accordingly, there was never a question of me not cooperating. Zarpa's English was severely limited and my Spanish had never earned more than a C in high school, but he was able to make clear what would happen should I fail to do exactly as he instructed.

The plan was simple. Zarpa inserted a cassette in the Sony and pressed the RECORD button. I spoke, addressing myself to Famous Floyd Chilly. The message was a straightforward lie.

"Graham is alive," I was made to say into the machine. "Give Zarpa anything he wants. Give him money, jewelry, anything of value."

We had a long recording session, Zarpa and I. He found it amusing to use the machete as a kind of conductor's baton. The cuts were superficial. Skindeep. Cross hatches, straight cuts, and the smooth, skater's curve of an engraver. It was not that the cuts caused that much pain—more a sort of scratch that burned as it bled. But the coldness of the blade seemed to penetrate to my bones until I was shivering, shivering.

And screaming, of course. Not with my own voice. The thing who screamed for Zarpa was not T. D. Stash of Key West, Florida. The thing who screamed was a mouth in a painting by Edvard Munch, the disembodied eye of Salvador Dalí, the mysterious shadow in a de Chirico landscape. The scream had a self of its own, and Zarpa made it live inside me.

It's never easy dealing with a perfectionist, and Zarpa made me repeat various versions of the same basic demand. "Your son is alive, pay up." Holding the razor edge of the blade against my throat, smiling slightly, so that just the white tips of his teeth were visible in the lantern light, he held the RECORD button down. I repeated the plea, striving to please him. Wanting to get it right. Then he would hit REWIND, play it back, rewind it, and I would do it again. And again.

While I begged him he stroked my face with the backs of his fingernails. For some reason I feared that more than the machete. Finally, when my voice was so hoarse I could barely whisper, he shut the cassette machine off. The slight smile widened into a grin, a murderous Cheshire floating in the darkness. He began tapping me with the blade, absentmindedly, as if tapping the end of a pencil against a desk top. Every tap cut me ever so slightly.

He had what he wanted. My usefulness, I supposed, was over. At that moment, lying on the hard ground in a congealing pool of my own blood, I did not fear death. I did not think of it. My mind was numb to everything but the fear of waiting, of anticipating each sequential heartbeat, each shallow breath. It was a fear that seeped from dreams of racial memory: of saber-toothed tigers, of rogue lions in the dark savanna.

I was the claw-pierced mouse, Zarpa the grinning cat.

After while he stood up, the machete at his side. He prodded me with his bare toes, as if curious to see how I'd react.

"Bien criado," he said. "Good boy."

Then the foot pushed violently and I was rolled over, facedown. I shut my eyes and thought of a white sailboat on an azure sea. I was able to fill the sails with wind. I concentrated on holding that image—white sails and languid green swells—ignoring the idea of the blade that was, surely, about to descend.

What Zarpa did was lace his fingers through the ropes and drag me facedown to the water's edge, where he bound me to a sturdy mangrove root with a length of galvanized chain, and left. From the other side of the tiny island came the sound of *Bushwhacked*'s engine coughing to life.

When the noise of the boat faded, I was alone, almost. Through the green veil of leaves a dead boy's eyes watched me.

I slept. A profound exhaustion ebbed in. The glimpse of the dead eyes I'd seen through the mangrove leaves made me want to inhale sleep like a puff of opium. I began to drift, strength utterly depleted, unable to feel or react.

Good boy, the voice of naked self intoned, you have played your part. Now sleep, and let the body heal, the spirit return.

Even as I floated, part of me knew the thing most likely to return was Zarpa.

Wake up, sleepy head, that part of me argued, set yourself free. You have miles to go, and promises to keep.

Useless to resist. I had no more strength than a kitten, how could I set myself free? These were nonsense notions, misplaced hope. Better to drift down into the comforting dark.

You have no mass, no weight, no reason to wake. So rest you easy and sleep. In sleep there is no fear, no pain, no grinning saber-tooth. Sleep . . . sleep . . . sleeeeeep . . .

I slept.

The white heron woke me. I had been aware of it as a figment of sleep, a white metaphor of dreamless peace. Standing on one leg in the shallows, it fixed me with a glittering eye. A not-so-ancient mariner hunting for the silver splash of a fish, or the side scuttle of a sand crab. Or anything that gleamed in the first, faint blush of dawn.

What gleamed, apparently, was a link in the chain that bound me to the mangroves. I felt a sudden, jabbing pressure in my wrists. That made me open my eyes. When the pale, sharp point of the heron beak flashed down, jabbing the bright chain, my first thought was that Zarpa had returned with his machete.

I jerked sideways. My legs came off the bank and splashed the water. Startled but not greatly disturbed, the great white backed off a few yards. It arched its wings like a white cloak and gazed at me first with one eye, then the other.

"Hello, bird," I heard myself whisper. "*¿Qué pasa?*"

What had happened was that the heron, a full-grown specimen four or five feet in height—most of it legs—had come looking for breakfast and found me instead.

Too large to eat, too immobilized to threaten, I was a curiosity. If I kicked wildly enough or screamed, no doubt the heron would seek breakfast elsewhere. I did neither. The bird was a thing of beauty, and it soothed me as sleep had not.

"Try the bonefish," I whispered. "Tide's rising. Bonefish coming in to feed."

The heron seemed to cock an ear, listening. It tucked up one leg and stood in a foot of water, as patient as time itself.

Where the predawn sky and the horizon met was a mist of translucent blue and indigo. Faint daubs of light twinkled, too low to be stars. A bridge, I assumed, somewhere along A-1-A. Maybe the run between Saddlebunch and Sugarloaf keys. Not that it mattered. The damp little island I shared with the great white heron and the dead boy was a good five miles into the bay. Fully rested and in tip-top shape, that was a lot farther than I could swim, even supposing I contrived to free myself before Zarpa returned.

If he returned.

By then I was awake enough to ponder why he'd left me alive. As insurance, in case he wanted another string of lies recorded for Floyd Chilly? Or was I simply one of the things he'd collected for his camp, like the shiny pots and pans?

There was one prospect I hadn't considered: that he was saving me for his pleasure. An extended game with the machete. That brought me as suddenly full awake as an injection of crystal Methedrine.

It made sense, or it might make sense to a twisted psychopath. Greed made him hurry away to Palmetto Key, where he intended to use the cassette of my voice as a lever to pry what he could from the Chillys. That accomplished, he would come back and kill me at his leisure. Slowly and deliberately.

Zarpa was an artist. His medium was pain. He would know how to keep the object of his experiment alive, barely, for quite some time.

I rattled the chain. The heron flapped its wings, as if scratching an itch. I stopped moving. Something in me didn't want to lose the bird. I admired its poise and balance, its uncanny ability to stalk and catch even the quickest of fish, stabbing with its daggerlike bill.

Not so long ago a heron, striding along A-1-A, was hit by a car. The motorist, remorseful, brought the great bird to a vet I know, hoping he could set its broken wing. The bird, he told me, seemed impervious to the pain it must have felt. As he prepared to sedate it, the impassive heron plucked out his left eye so cleanly that he never saw it move, or felt the extraction.

The heron, as it happened, died. My friend the vet now has a very pretty glass eye that he will remove and roll down the bar when an excess of rum moves him. Understandably, he now declines to treat wounded herons, although he bears them no particular animus.

An idea formed. I grabbed it and held on.

"Hey, doc," I whispered to the bird, "come on over. See the shiny fish?"

I wiggled the chain where it looped through the submerged mangrove roots. The bird folded its wings against its body and watched with one eye.

I worked the chain slowly, letting the links turn and twist, hoping they caught the dim morning light, as it must have when the bird first woke me.

In the back of my mind Mutt Durgin was chortling on his fat cigar. You fishin' for heron now, boy? Finally given up on them big tarpon?

I know what I'm doing.

Don't know shit from Shinola, son.

I'm going to set myself free, Mutt. Before Zarpa comes back to play with me.

Granted, I wasn't thinking clearly. Torture does that to you. That and the oppressive stink of death. But I knew enough to appeal to the bird's instinct. I knew about lures and tricks of light. I knew about stealth and cunning and patience. Especially the art of patience. You need a lot of that in the guide business, not so much for the fish as for the men who hire you to find them.

The heron approached, inching through the shallows so cautiously it seemed hardly to move. My rope-bound hands were just beneath the surface of the water, drawing the slack of the chain along the mangrove root. I kept my eyes averted, not wanting to distract it from the tantalizing glitter of the chain.

Pretty fishy. Come to spear the pretty fishy.

Observed from the prone position, a great white looks about ten feet tall. The beak is as long and sharp as a broadsword. Remembering what happened to my friend the vet, I turned my face away and worked the chain by touch.

Pretty fishy. See it shine? See it turn?

The heron struck three times. The first two blows rattled the chain and pierced the mangrove root. The third strike pierced the palm of my left hand. A saltwater stigmata that hurt like hell. I roared, yanking against the chain. The bird shrieked and staggered away. I felt its great wings brush my head.

And then I was sitting up in the shallow water with the heavy chain in my lap, looking at where the mangrove root had been cleanly severed. The heron looked at me with great disdain before launching into ungainly flight. It swooped low over the bay, wings trailing in the water, and vanished into the advancing fog as I struggled to untie the ropes.

Free at last, dizzy and reeling, I ravaged the camp like a honey-drunk bear, flinging pots and pans about. Kicking over fuel cans, yanking at the tarpaulin. Looking for a weapon. What I wanted, to settle the shaky fear in my belly, was a large-caliber automatic weapon. Something that would be lethal well out of machete range.

What I found, under the camp stove, was a flimsy fish-filleting knife. Of the disposable type, with a white plastic handle. It was not exactly a BAR machine gun, but having it made me feel better.

I tore a strip from my tattered shirt and cinched it tight over where the heron had poked a hole in the palm of my hand. I was hurting in so many places one more wound didn't make much difference.

The next thing I required was food. I was trembling with the need of it, despite the awful stench coming from the place in the mangroves I had studiously avoided. Surely Zarpa, that twisted Boy Scout, would keep a stock of goodies in his hideout? I tore through the rubble with visions of freeze-dried food rations and found instead a small tin of sugar and a skinny tube of processed sausage. A fucking Slim Jim. I ate a handful of the sugar, gagged, and tore the plastic from the sausage. The rush from the sugar hit me and I could hardly hold on to the greasy piece of meat. Protein, of a sort.

I tried, but the bits of fat in the sausage looked like something alive. I flung it away and concentrated on keeping the sugar down. After the shaking came under control, I got up and started toward the far end of the key, as far away as I could get from the thing in the mangroves. I didn't get more than a couple of yards before tripping over a fuel can.

"Son of a bitch!" I hit at the can with my bad hand. Tears of rage stung the cuts on my cheeks.

In the funny papers a light bulb goes on overhead when an idea flashes to mind. It was like that with me, only I imagined a fire instead of a light bulb. Zarpa had burned me out of the mangroves once, when he came after the counterfeit payoff. Turning the tables on him would be a pleasure. Of more immediate concern, a bonfire might attract attention to this desolate part of the bay.

In my weakened state I functioned best by concentrating on a single notion or object. A weapon, a bandage, then food. Now I focused all of my feeble energy on a quest for fire.

With six gallons of high-grade, camp-stove kerosene at hand, making a fire seemed a reasonable-enough objective. I found matches in my pants pocket. Soaking wet, they dissolved like sticky bits of pink candy.

I looked everywhere in that wretched camp. In the

collection of little tin cans, under and around the camp stove. The Coleman lantern. I distinctly remembered the flare as Zarpa ignited the lantern. What had he used? A lighter? A kitchen match? A flint sparker?

Maybe the son of a bitch had rubbed two sticks together. Whatever he used, he had clearly taken it with him.

I felt so frustrated I wanted to bang my forehead against the ground, except it was the one part of me that didn't hurt. I went to my knees and tried to think of a reason not to ask a certain question.

The question was this: "Hey, Graham, got a light?"

The cool morning fog had thickened. Ghostly wisps of it trailed through the mangroves. God how I hated mangroves. Gathering the remains of my strength, I took a deep breath and held it.

The branches were heavy and brittle. Cutting through them was machete work, but I didn't have a machete. I pulled each leaf-laden branch back until it snapped, tearing at the resilient flesh of the mangrove trunk. My whole being was concentrated on the work of pulling the branches free. I didn't want to think beyond the work. I didn't want to think at all.

Quit with the hide-and-seek, Graham, I know you're in there.

I wrenched at the branches, taking short, chugging breaths of the heavy air.

Come on out, Graham. All-ee all-ee en-tree.

He was waiting patiently under the shroud of leaves. When I pulled the last branch away, I saw that the eyes I'd glimpsed from the shore were not eyes at all, but small shiny things feasting where his eyes had been.

Some things are not as bad as you think they'll be. Some are worse. Searching the pockets of the dead boy was worse, much worse. In the tropics the dead spoil rapidly, and Graham had been gone for a couple of days, maybe longer. His flesh had swollen, bloating the thin body and tearing the seams of his shirt and pants. The fingers, those that had not been servered from his hands in the course of Zarpa's machete game, looked like spoiled sausages.

Thinking of the Slim Jim I'd almost eaten, I started to giggle.

It was the kind of laughter that if you don't get hold of it, never stops. I forced myself to look at the boy's face and the panicky feeling passed. I could see where the ear had been removed. Curiously, there was little blood. As if Graham had been dead before the ear was taken. What was I thinking? This wasn't Graham I was looking at. No way. Graham had shuffled off his mortal coil.

Graham Chilly doesn't live there anymore, Stash. What you're looking at is a piece of rotten fruit.

The sweet, gassy stench of him seemed to suck all life from the air. It took every erg of willpower to turn him over. Alive he hadn't weighed more than a hundred and twenty pounds. Dead he was a ton or more of absolute dread.

But there in the pocket I cut from the swollen seat of his jeans was a cigarette lighter. A Bic disposable, with plenty of butane visible through the translucent plastic case.

God bless you, Baron Bich. You are forgiven for your cheap, leaky pens.

The timber framework of the old camp was punky and rotten. Not exactly ideal bonfire material. But stacked in the clearing and soaked with enough kerosene, it burned. The smell of a hot, lively fire was a relief. To keep it going I tore the cedar foundation posts from the ground. When I judged the blaze bright enough, I threw in the wadded-up tarpaulin. Great billows of smoke went up, black and sooty. I cut wet mangrove leaves with the filleting knife and tossed them on the flames.

"Smoke, you bugger, smoke."

Smoke it did. Finally I had to retreat to the water. Exhausted, eyes partially blinded with the acrid smoke, I had a pleasant little fantasy about being rescued by the Coast Guard. A chopper would appear overhead and one of those lovely female ensigns from the Marathon station would rapelle down a rope and take me away. Abroad the chopper they would feed me hot chocolate and bind my wounds as I slept.

It was a compelling fantasy, real enough so I almost didn't hear the distant thumping of marine engines. For a while I thought I was imagining things, that what I heard was merely the exaggerated beat of my heart. Then the thrumming became deeper. Not imagination, but a pair of twin diesels.

I searched the white mist. The water lapped around my knees. From behind me the smoke billowed outward. I opened my mouth to shout and produced a few hoarse, nearly inhuman bellows. Naked ape noises: Find me, please.

When the gray silhouette of a commercial fishing hull formed in the fog, I was struck by a horrible thought. What if it was Zarpa coming home in style? Suppose he had traded *Bushwhacked* in for a bigger, faster vessel? Who but Zarpa would have reason to check out this godforsaken mangrove patch in the middle of Florida Bay?

Holding tight to the pathetic little filleting knife, I backed up to the shoreline. The boat that emerged was a new white gill-netter. A burly redhead in the stern pointed at me and shouted. By then my voice wasn't working, so I responded by waving my arms.

That's how I got rescued by Zach Malone.

After handing me a blanket, the son I thought of as Popeye turned to his father and said, "Will you lookit him, Paw? Appears like he got et by a whale and then spit out, don't he?"

Malone turned the helm over to his other son and brought me a mug of coffee. It was as hot and sweet as a night in August, and I held on to it for dear life.

"You been cut up pretty bad," Zach said. "Lost some blood. How'd that crazy greaser get the jump on you?"

I told him, briefly. He nodded, expressing neither sympathy nor condescension. The same attitude he might have directed toward a fellow smuggler who ran into a killing storm.

"We comin' back from Naples when Roy saw the smoke over Billy Goat Key," he said. "Used to be a fishing camp on there in the old days. I figured maybe some kids got out and set the place afire."

"Only me."

"You ever find that boy? The one whose daddy sings those old songs on the teevee?"

"I found him," I said.

The small green eyes blinked. "Pretty bad, huh?" he asked.

"Bad enough. I'd be obliged, Zach, if you'd turn on that marine radio over there and put a call through to Lieutenant Nelson Kerry, of the Key West police."

Six green eyes stared me down.

"I say we throw him over, Paw," Popeye said.

"They figure to home on the signal," Roy said, smirking at me from the helm. "Him and that DEA asshole drives the red Porsche."

Zach didn't respond. He just kept lookin at me, like my forehead was made of glass and he could read my thoughts.

"Them cuts is prob'ly makeup." Popeye was mighty pleased with himself for thinking of the idea. "Like they do in the movies, right? He ain't hurt at all."

I looked to the rear of the boat. The open cockpit was empty, just mopped clean. But there was canvas over the ice hatch and a loop of rope holding it tight. I wondered what contraband they might be carrying from Naples, or if that had really been their point of departure. Not enough space down there for a decent cargo of weed, and anyhow they were traveling in the wrong direction for that.

"We been up to the bank," Zach said slowly, as if testing the sound of his own voice. "Made a withdrawal."

Popeye snatched the empty coffeecup from my hands and threw it overboard, where it vanished in the wake. "Don't tell him nuthin', Paw."

"Shut up," his father said. "They just lookin' out for family," he explained to me. "Some reason or other, they don't trust you, Stash. Think you mix with the wrong kind of people."

"Look here," I said, "I don't give a flying fuck how much money you've got in that ice hatch. I don't care if it's filled to the scuppers with cocaine, or South African diamonds, or powdered rhino horn. I just want someone to warn Floyd Chilly."

Zach and his boys mulled it over as the gill-netter ran southeast on autopilot, making a course for the Stock Island channel. The fog thickened as we approached the main islands. The early-morning sun was barely visible as a halo through the white mist. Spooky weather, the kind that made you want to hang an extra radar deflector from the masthead.

Except Malone wasn't carrying any radar deflectors, for the simple reason that he didn't want to be picked up on anyone's screen, not if he could help it. Not with whatever it was he had stored in that ice hatch. Too risky. And he wasn't, as he explained, a fellow who knowingly took a risk.

"We'll be pleased to drop you where you want to go," he said. "After that we'll give the lieutenant a call."

"It may be too late by then. Might be too late now."

"Best we can do."

If it weren't for his two boys, I think Zach would have gone along with me. Or maybe that was just the impression he wanted to leave me with. Whatever, I sensed it was pointless to argue. When we raised the dock at Palmetto Key I left the cabin and went out on deck. I could make out the *Golden Oldie* where it was tied up to the pilings, and the edge of the manicured lawn. I could almost see the caretaker's cottage, but the main house was behind the white bank of fog.

Zach followed me out to the deck as his boat came alongside the dock.

"Here's a couple things might come in handy," he said.

He handed me a cotton shirt. It was Malone-sized, which meant there was plenty of room inside for me. The other thing he gave me was a .44 Magnum. The very same cannon he'd pulled that night above his saloon when I'd walked in without an invitation.

"You're smart, you won't get near enough to that crazy bastard to cut him with that little knife. You all just point this at him and keep pulling the trigger."

I took the big, flashy gun and thanked him. "You sure you don't want to come along, just for the fun of it?"

"I'd love to," he said, "excepting I'm real busy right now."

I swung over the side and landed with both feet

on Floyd Chilly's dock. The gill-netter reversed, then glided off, fading white on white. As I headed up the path toward the main house, I noticed that something was wrong with my knees. They were shaking.

21

THE fog did funny things to the neon flamingo. The mist around it was charged with an unreal pink light, as if the bird inhabited an atmosphere all its own. The way the useless neon wing flapped made it look like a stage prop in a Beckett play, absurd and enigmatic. Like a lot of things that end up in Key West.

Circling up to the main house, I kept close to the shore, figuring that Zarpa might have hidden *Bush-whacked* out of habit, or possibly missed the dock in the fog. Not that there was any certainty he would come by water. That depended where he took Paula Davis, and what he did to her, a prospect I didn't care to contemplate right then.

Handling a .44 Magnum is like pumping iron. You have to fight gravity to keep it leveled. As a target pistol it is fine, except for the mule-kick recoil. As a weapon it has all the convenience of a twenty-pound Swiss Army knife. Neither drawback has adversely affected its popularity in southern Florida, where Dirty Harry is considered a sentimental realist, and Grandma has a thing for Uzis.

What it boils down to, the .44 Mag has sex appeal. Which doesn't make a lot of sense, since it takes both hands to keep it up.

That said, I was mighty glad of the company. Only the day before I had been prepared to shoot

Zarpa if absolutely necessary. Playtime on Billy Goat Key had changed all that. Now it was absolutely necessary to shoot him first and question it later, if ever. Pure, unadulterated fear had emptied me of moral reservations. It had emptied me of everything except the profound desire never to be in his power again.

Keep shooting, Zach Malone had advised. Sounded reasonable enough to me.

I'm not sure what I expected to find inside the main house. A nightmare surprise, maybe, if Zarpa had already arrived. I wasn't ready for rock-a-billy guitar licks or bourbon fumes. I was aware of both as I stood at the open door. No locks or bolts, no one to answer my tentative knock. What had happened to security?

The answer was passed out in the foyer. Carlos, his uniform stained with vomit, was curled up on the quarry-tile floor. He smelled like he'd been brewed and bonded in Kentucky. When I pushed him with my foot, he whimpered like a child having a bad dream. I left him there and moved toward the source of the music.

The song was an old Eddie Cochran tune, "Summertime Blues," but it didn't sound like Eddie Cochran or any of his rock-a-billy imitators. It sounded like Floyd Chilly, expressing his intention to raise a holler about the indignity of having to work all summer in pursuit of a dollar. He was perched on a stool at the bar, in close proximity to an opened bottle of bourbon. He had an acoustic guitar on his knee and he was fingerpicking and slapping the strings.

"Do do do do," he sang, "da da da da."

The gravelly voice was fine and strong. I was impressed. The booze gave him a raw edge that was missing in his Famous-Floyd-covers-hits-by-other-artists persona. No wonder he'd had such a struggle kicking the alcohol habit.

I hadn't considered what my personal appearance might do to someone who wasn't expecting me. The glass slipped from Floyd's fingers as he lifted the drink to his lips.

"Jesus," he sighed, "I thought you was a dead man, for just a second there."

I sat down on a stool and rested the Magnum on the bar. "You fell off the wagon," I said.

"Nah," he said, pouring into a new glass. "What I did, I jumped." He took the bourbon straight, without so much as a wince. "Goddamn. What happened to you?"

I told him about Zarpa and my excursion to Billy Goat Key. His bloodshot eyes blinked slowly as he sipped and listened. I could see where the booze changed more than just his voice. There was a meanness around his mouth I hadn't noticed before, and a hard, opaque glint in his eye.

"I've got bad news, Floyd," I said, coming to the end. "The worst kind."

His hand, moving in slow motion to the bottle, halted. "The boy is dead," he said dully. "I know that already. The cop called, the one who's a friend of yours. Told me the coroner says Graham was expired before that ear was cut off."

"It was quick," I lied. "I'm pretty sure he never felt a thing."

He nodded, poured from the bottle. If my guess was right, the bourbon had been the first thing Floyd reached for after hearing about the coroner's conclusion. Which reminded me. I picked up the ghastly pink telephone and dialed Lieutenant Kerry at his home number. His wife answered and informed me that Nelly had just received a call and was responding to it.

"Do you know where he was headed?" I asked.

"All he said, going out the door, was some jerk was in trouble and he had to back him up."

"Some jerk?" I said.

"His exact words."

I apologized for disturbing her and hung up, hoping I was the jerk Nelly had gone to back up.

Floyd continued to fritter around on the guitar, as if he hadn't quite connected to what was going down. As if he didn't give a damn what happened, or to whom. "I'm a gonna raise a fuss," he sang huskily. "I'm a gonna raise a holler."

I put my hand over the strings. The whiskey meanness around his mouth hardened. "I heard something out there," I said. "Give it a listen."

There it was. The bee drone of an boat engine. Floyd grunted and looked out the picture window. The sun was beginning to rise overhead, but the low fog was thick enough so the shoreline was obscured in mist. Taking the .44 with me, I moved to the patio door and stood there listening. The way sound distorts as it carries over water made it hard to tell if the engine was a mile away or only a few hundred yards. I thought it sounded like *Bushwhacked*'s outboard drive, but I didn't trust my senses. I was ready to hear Zarpa in any sound that came my way.

Floyd Chilly sang in an ugly monotone, "If I was a rich man, ya-de-de-da-de-de-da-de." Twisting the lyrics into a vocal sneer of self-loathing. He stood up, holding the guitar by the neck like he meant to throttle it. There was a loud thumping from the direction of the foyer. Someone banging on the front door.

I could see the door rattling the jam. It was being kicked, hard. Disturbed by the noise, Carlos stirred, covering his face with the crook of his arm.

"You open up," Regina Chilly screamed. "Floyd, you bastard, open this door!"

I told him to draw the bolt and stand back quickly while I covered.

He looked at me like I was crazy. "Go ahead and shoot her," he said. "Might get her attention."

I explained my concern that Zarpa might be out there, that he should get his wife inside immediately. What with the swearing and the slamming, I couldn't tell whether the boat engine was still droning from the bay.

Regina Chilly was alone. She threw her handbag at Floyd and rushed at him, pummeling with her fists, her face a mask of hate. I listened at the open door and heard the boat engine throttle down and then stop. In the neighborhood, definitely.

"Break it up," I said, bolting the door. "We haven't got much time."

It wasn't much of a brawl as matrimonial battles go. Reggie was hitting Floyd and he was standing there and taking it. I could see where his knuckles were white on the neck of the guitar, but he never raised his hands. The punches he threw came from his eyes and Reggie was trying to claw at them when I grabbed her wrists.

"You can settle this later. I think we're about to have company, okay? The gentleman who murdered your son wants to make a social call."

Carlos was on his knees. His face was the color of dead grass. "*Borracho*," he moaned. "*Muy borracho.*"

Things were just peachy. I had a booze-soaked client, his hysterical wife, and a sick-drunk security guard to deal with before getting ready for whatever madness Zarpa had planned. It was like a nightmare game of *Beat the Clock*, with me herding Reggie into the kitchen and ordering her to stay out of sight, and Floyd singing a bawdy song about a Mexican whorehouse while he helped his "little buddy" Carlos into the nearest bathroom. The choreography was definitely ragged. I left Reggie going through her purse in a panic, looking for God knows what, and Carlos making mewling noises as he hugged the commode.

"He don't have a lot of experience with hard stuff," Floyd confided. "I been givin' him lessons."

The door bell chimed. It played the first few notes of a maddeningly familiar tune, over and over. Whoever was at the door had a finger on the button and wasn't letting go.

"Hang on," Floyd shouted in a singsong voice. "I'm comin'!"

There was a coat closet opposite the door. I got into it and left the sliders open just wide enough so I could see and not be seen. Floyd grinned at me and tipped an imaginary hat. Like he was having a splendid time. As he drew back the bolt and clicked the lock, I thought, Well, maybe it's my old buddy Nelson Kerry, come to the rescue.

It wasn't Nellie, though. It was Zarpa, wearing a new guayabera shirt, clean chinos, and a pair of sandals. Looking fresh-scrubbed and all duded up, like he wanted to make a good impression.

My finger tightened on the trigger just as Floyd shifted, getting in my line of sight.

"What you all want," he said. "You a friend of Graham's, is that it?"

Over Floyd's shoulder I could see Zarpa nod happily.

"If I'm not mistaken," Floyd said, "that's my boy's radio. You gonna tell me how you got hold of it?"

Zarpa had the boom box with him. I could see where there was the shape of a pistol under the guayabera. The .38 he'd taken off me. I looked for the machete but couldn't see it. Had to be there, somewhere. He couldn't leave it out of reach.

"Ain't you got nothin' to say for yourself?" Floyd asked. "Whatsa matter, cat got your tongue?"

I think Zarpa understood, because he grinned and gestured with the boom box. I hadn't had time to tell Floyd about the recording session at Billy Goat Key, featuring T. D. Stash begging for his life. That was what I was expecting to hear when Zarpa pushed the PLAYBACK button.

I wasn't ready for the screaming. Either Zarpa had put the wrong side of the cassette in the machine, or else he was crazy enough to want to torment Floyd Chilly with the sounds of Graham pleading for a quick death. The volume was on high, blasting out of the speakers. It was as if the boy was there in the room with us, terrified, screaming to stop, stop stop, and please kill me quick, oh pleeeeease.

The effect was stunning. Floyd staggered, as if hit by a blow. Zarpa was starting to punch at one of the tape-recorder buttons when Floyd reached out and grabbed his neck with his big plowman's hands. He squeezed. Floyd's bulk blocked most of what I could see, but it was obvious that Zarpa was turning purple.

I charged from the closet, looking for a place to shoot. From there on things got more confused. Zarpa had dropped the boom box when Floyd started to throttle him, but Graham's dying mantra didn't stop. Regina came out of the kitchen, hands covering her ears, matching her son scream for scream. Carlos was right behind her, skidding drunkenly on the quarry tiles.

There are six shots in a .38 Smith & Wesson. Five of them went into Floyd Chilly, killing him as he stood. One of them, a ricochet, hit Carlos just below the left knee. He went down like a hammered calf.

All I can remember is the look on his face, twisted up in the kind of silent, Spanish agony Picasso put in *Guernica*. I had only a glimpse of him before Floyd came tumbling back, his deadweight knocking me down, kicking the wind out of me.

Graham stopped screaming, or the tape ended. Reggie kept right on, carrying the same high pitch. I shoved my way out from under Floyd, covered with his blood, trying to catch my breath. Zarpa threw the empty gun at me. I ducked and he grabbed Reggie and yanked her out the door.

Right about then the Cavalry arrived. Lieutenant Nelson Kerry, laying on the siren and spraying gravel as his cruiser slid to a stop. I was on my hands and knees, hanging on to the .44 as I crawled through the door, and my schoolboy chum Nellie damn near shot me.

There was a spark of recognition, an instinctive flinch that made him lift the weapon. Still fighting for air, I nodded and pointed in the direction Zarpa had fled. He hadn't got far because Reggie was putting up one hell of a struggle, kicking and flailing as he dragged her backward, toward the dock.

The machete had been there all along, hanging from a lanyard between his shoulder blades. He yanked back Reggie's chin and held the blade to her throat. She responded by sinking her teeth into his wrist.

He howled and let her go. Reggie fell to the ground and curled into a fetal position, chewing on her knuckles. I could see the whites of her eyes, the glittering madness in them. Kerry got off a shot just as Zarpa sprinted toward the water. Then it was a footrace. Zarpa in the lead, one arm hanging where he'd been nicked by the bullet, followed by Nelson Kerry, followed by me.

Zarpa was fastest by far. What got him was geography. Palmetto Key just wasn't big enough. He got to the end of it and there was nowhere else to go. The fog was especially thick right at the water's edge. Kerry, about ten yards ahead of me, pulled up short as he got to the dock. Zarpa sprang out of the mist, the machete flashing in a downward arc.

I fired and missed. Kerry fired and hit him, rolling sideways as the blade came down. Zarpa, gut-shot, bellowed. His voice was high and keening. He staggered backward, the dock boards clanging under his feet. He'd lost one of the sandals. There was blood on his bare foot.

I steadied myself and fired again. The .44 kicked, nearly jumping out of my hand. Wood splintered behind Zarpa. From the ground Kerry fired again, from a range of maybe ten feet. Zarpa spun with the impact, but did not lose his balance. He raised the machete over his head and ran to keep from falling. At the end of the dock he half-fell, half-leapt onto the stern of the *Golden Oldie*, the sport-fishing machine Floyd Chilly had signed over to me. He dropped over the gunwhale and out of sight.

Kerry was back on his feet. He screamed at me to stay back. Later he told me he'd thought, from the blood smeared all over me, that I'd been badly shot and was just too dumb to know it. I screamed that Zarpa was going to get away, although I knew perfectly well the keys were not in the ignition. They were in my desk drawer, where'd I'd left them, along with the hull documentation.

In the heat of the moment I thought Zarpa capable of anything. I thought he was a thing that would not die, no matter how many of Nelson Kerry's bullets tore into him. The truth of the matter is, the fear of him was still inside me. And the clawhold of fear did not let go until Nellie grabbed me and said,

"Stop shooting, you asshole. You're putting holes in the goddamn boat."

I was up on the stern, trying to draw a bead on where Zarpa, in his dying agony, had crawled up under the pedestal of the fighting chair. I squeezed the trigger one more time. It clicked, empty. None of my shots hit Zarpa, who was dead by then, but I put four half-inch holes in the starboard fuel tanks.

It was diesel fuel flowing out that Kerry saw, not water flowing in.

"Help me get him off of here before the boat fucking burns," he said.

He was mad as hell when I wouldn't give him a hand with Zarpa's body. No way was I going to touch him. I'd sooner have swum naked in the Everglades, among the gators. When I saw one of his hands spasm, those horny claws curling down in a postmortem muscle spasm, it was all I could do to keep from throwing the empty gun at him.

By then the *Golden Oldie* was starting to smolder. I thought about going aboard and trying to douse the fire. But a couple of hundred gallons of fuel had flowed in the bilge, and although diesel grade is slow to ignite, it will burn hot and the fumes are deadly. So I turned my back on the boat and followed Kerry off the dock as he dragged Zarpa's body by the ankles, roundly cursing me for being such a bonehead.

"You ought to see yourself," he grunted, giving the body a yank as it came off the dock planking. "Hell, I've seen better-looking corpses. And another thing, I'm not taking the blame for setting the boat on fire."

"Don't worry about it, I'll handle it."

I was ashamed to tell him it had been my vessel, briefly. I didn't want to turn and look. The heat on my back told me all I needed to know about what was happening as the tanks ruptured and the superstructure caught fire.

"Yeah, you'll handle it." He dropped Zarpa's lifeless legs. "Jesus, T. D., you're bleeding all over. You sure he didn't shoot you?"

"Pretty sure," I said. There were sirens up by the main house, and lights flashing weird in the fog. "You're not going to like this, Nel, but we got to go look for the girl."

"What girl?"

I told him about Paula Davis and the houseboat where she lived and painted. Kerry swore again and then turned and kicked dirt at Zarpa's corpse. That sounds like unnecessary cruelty, I know, but you'd a had to have been there.

22

THAT same ornery pelican was strutting the deck of the *Green Flash* when we got to Coral Canal. Kerry drove the cruiser as far as it would go into the overgrown access road. We hiked in the last hundred yards, through the stagnant pools and the decaying concrete and the ruination that happens when Mother Nature gets together with real-estate developers.

When we were hip-deep in the loathsome mangroves, Nellie looked over at me and shook his head. "Goddamn, bubba," he said. "You look like something left over from a *Dawn of the Dead* film."

"I've had better days," I said, yanking my foot from the greedy mud and slime. "On the whole, I'd rather be in Philadelphia."

The dinghy was tied up to the houseboat, out in the channel. We were discussing the pros and cons of swimming out—there were no pros, really—when Nellie spotted the aluminum canoe where it had drifted up against the shore. As we got into it and pushed off, I was thinking that Zarpa had moved up, boatwise. In less than twenty-four hours he'd gone from a beat-up canoe to a custom guide boat, and then briefly staked a claim on a high-ticket sportfisherman. Only in America, land of opportunity, like the song said.

Kerry had a way with pelicans. He faked a swing

at it with the canoe paddle and the thing took off, humping wings to gain altitude.

"Here goes nothing," Kerry said, pulling himself aboard the *Green Flash* and opening the screen door.

I followed him into the dim interior, still holding the empty Magnum. I was feeling light-headed, and the weight of it helped ground me to reality. Reality was that we found Paula Davis facedown under the galley table.

Kerry turned her over and loosened the gag from her mouth.

"Thirsty," she said, and coughed.

I found a beer in the ice chest while Kerry cut her loose from the nest of rope. She gulped down half the can while we explained what had happened at Palmetto Key.

"I thought you were past tense, for sure," she said to me. "When Zarpa came back to the boat, he had blood all over his hands."

She told us how he had taken her back to the houseboat, where he had partially untied her and demanded that she make a picture of him. That sounded crazy, but no crazier than anything else he'd done. Paula showed us the pile of wadded-up sketches she'd gone through before working the jitters out of her hand.

"I figured, this was it. I'd do him and then he'd do me, right? He's sitting there bare-chested, posing with that precious machete. I'm noticing the blood on the edge of the blade. It's kind of a burnt sienna when it dries. And you know what he says to me. Zarpa? He wants, he says *hazme ver como un rico*. Make me look like a rich man. Can you believe it?"

At that moment I believed anything. I believed that ten thousand angels danced on the head of a pin, that the moon was made of green cheese, that Richard Nixon wasn't a crook.

My pal the lieutenant was staring at Paula's portrait the way he used to stare at comic books, with total absorption. It was a vivid watercolor, a splash of browns and blacks and glinting whites, accented with pen and ink. The likeness was uncanny. In the picture Zarpa looked powerful, frightening, as he had in life. Paula had made his long fingernails even more talonlike, where they curved around the machete handle. As if his nails were the place where the beast in him was made manifest. The demon tearing through.

"It's almost beautiful," I said.

Paula shuddered. She took the stiff sheet of paper from Kerry and tore it in half, then in quarters, and so on, until Zarpa's last picture was a handful of confetti.

"After I did him, he uses that shower I rigged up. Washes his hair with my shampoo, okay? Then he comes out here, naked as a jaybird, and just stands over me. I figure, this is it, now he's going to rape me."

"Did he?" Kerry wanted to know.

"What he did," she said, "he stroked me with those awful fingernails. Real slow and gentle. Like I was a pet or something. It sounds weird, but I'd almost rather have been raped."

She threw the scraps of paper into the canal. A scattering of small white leaves on the stagnant water. The pelican had returned. You could hear his webbed feet pitter-pattering on deck.

"You guys know anyone wants to buy a houseboat?" Paula asked. "I just decided, I'm splitting to Arizona."

After it was over I went home and unplugged the

phone and got in my hammock, intending to sleep for a hundred years. In my dreams I imagined the hammock was a cocoon, that some momentous change would occur when finally I emerged from it. With any luck I would become a twenty-first-century man, with impervious vinyl skin, a heart of the purest titanium, and no nerves at all. I would never need to love, or fear, or dream.

When I woke up the wind was sighing through the screens, carrying the scent of frangipani blossoms and the faint, sulfurous smell of Key West Electric. I could hear the Conch Train cruising down Southard Street, powered by propane gas and traveler's checks. It was just another day in paradise and nothing much had changed, especially not me.

More than anything I wanted a long cool shower, but it was too much trouble washing around the streaks of mercurochrome the ER doctor had daubed all over me. I ended up just ducking my head and scrubbing under my arms, fisherman-style. There was nothing I could do about my face. I was stuck with it.

Old Man Sánchez was out in front of his *bodega*, sitting on an orange crate and smoking a fat cigar. He was too polite to comment on the purple streaks and bandages, or maybe he was just used to my shenanigans. I wished him a good evening and walked west until I bumped into Whitehead Street and the Green Parrot Bar on the corner.

"What'll it be?"

"Nepenthe," I said. "Straight up."

I settled for a beer and a shot, and had the pleasure of watching the bartender try to look up "nepenthe" in his mixer's handbook. I still had that maddening, dingdong melody going round in my head, from the door chimes at Floyd Chilly's estate, and I figured my best chance of finding it was to consult the Green Parrot's jukebox.

I scored on the third quarter: "Don't Fence Me In", the Cole Porter classic about being an old cowhand on the Rio Grande. The version on the juke was an oldie, with Bing Crosby backed by the Andrews Sisters. It suited me down to the ground, and I punched the combination until I ran out of change.

The second time around I convinced the bartender to sing along. We were declaring our aversion to hobbles and fences when Trudy came in. She was glowing like a madonna in a medieval painting.

"Hello, Nebraska. Nice ring you got there."

It seemed she and Duane were getting married. They were going back to Bowling Green, where he taught, and she was thinking of doing something really crazy, like have a baby.

"Nothing crazy about that," I said, grinning until it hurt. I don't think I fooled her, though. I hadn't fooled anyone lately.

Several drinks went by. Kurt Hansen sauntered in and insisted on buying a round. He was wearing enough gold chain to strangle an Inca and talking his usual ragtime about the rewards of a government job.

"You proved something to me, Stash my man. Anything I can do for you," he promised, eyes glinting, "all you gotta do is ask."

So I asked him to put a quarter in the juke and press the E-7 combination. After that he lost interest. The last I saw of him he was showing his red Porsche to a girl with orange hair. The color clash didn't seem to bother him, but what can you expect from a guy who wears sunglasses at night?

We sat on the stool until closing, me and Bing and the Andrews Sisters. I tried very hard not to think about the things I didn't want to think about. Like

Graham and Famous Floyd and the rubber-walled room where they had taken Regina, who kept hearing the scream long after the tape ran out.

I almost made it. Then I blew it by doing the thing you never do, if you're tough enough: I cried in my beer.

About the Author

Before turning to fiction, W. R. Philbrick covered the waterfront as a longshoreman and later as a boatbuilder. From time to time he has lived and worked in the Florida Keys, most recently aboard the *Caribaya*, a vessel he designed and built.

MYSTERY PARLOR

☐ **CHIAROSCURO by Peter Clothier.** Famous artist Jacob Molnar could afford to turn his back on the art world's phoniness ... but he can no longer turn away when he finds himself spinning in a very real kaleidoscope of crime, in which murder showed promise of becoming the most modern art—and he its next creation ... "Gripping!"—*Houston Chronicle* (148614—$3.50)

☐ **AN ADVANCEMENT OF LEARNING by Reginald Hill.** Murder on campus is academic when the corpse of the college president is found mouldering in a makeshift grave. And Inspectors Dalziel and Pascoe find the motives of a killer don't depend on book learning, but on the most common of all denominators— love and rage ... "Deadly wit ... Machiavellian plotting, sheer fun." (146565—$2.95)

☐ **A CADENZA FOR CARUSO by Barbara Paul.** Murder and blackmail stalk the Met and the great Enrico Caruso plays detective to clear his friend of the charges. But snooping leads to secrets behind the scener ... and if Caruso isn't careful, murder may take an encore ... "Thoroughly delightful!"—Publishers Weekly (145232—$2.95)

☐ **THE 600 POUND GORILLA by Robert Campbell.** When the boiler is the local zoo goes kaput, Chicago's favorite gorilla, Baby, gets transferred to a local hot spot. But things heat up when two customers are found beaten to death and everyone thinks Baby went bananas. But precinct captain Jimmy Flannery is about to risk his life to provei it's murder ... (147103—$2.95)

☐ **GOING, GOING, GONE by Eliza G.C. Collins.** An antiques auction contains something worth killing for ... But the gallery owner, framed for the murder, didn't do it. Now, her talent for investigation is the only thing that can preserve her freedom.... (149637—$2.95)

Buy them at your local
bookstore or use coupon
on next page for ordering.